THE BLINDNESS OF
SERGEANT CLUFF

Detective-Sergeant Cluff is at home in the bleak, moorland market town of 1960s Gunnarshaw. A gruff and gloomy loner, he has spent a lifetime observing local folk – and knows their lives inside out. They know him, too – a bulky, macintoshed figure who watches from the shadows of Gunnarshaw's ginnels as they go about their daily business, his dog Clive always at his side.

But it's not just criminals Cluff has to watch out for. Never satisfied with easy answers to cases, Cluff is a maverick and no flatterer to authority – much to the bemusement of Detective-Constable Barker, but much more so to the despair of the hapless Inspector Mole, who tries at every opportunity to outwit or contain Cluff's singular methods of detection.

But beneath Cluff's dour exterior beats the heart of a truly compassionate man who possesses a deep understanding of human nature, in all its sordid and depraved details – details which frequently push Cluff to bend the rules in his pursuit of moral justice.

Gil North's novels, which follow the investigations of Detective-Sergeant Cluff in the fictional and close-knit moorland market town of Gunnarshaw, were first published in the 1960s. Incredibly popular, they were adapted for BBC Television and regularly attracted twelve million viewers. Gil North wrote the scripts for every episode.

Gil North was the pen-name of Geoffrey Horne (1916–1988). He was born in Skipton, North Yorkshire, where his father was Town Clerk. Horne was educated at the local grammar school, then studied at Christ's College, Cambridge, before embarking on a career as a civil servant in Nigeria and Cameroon.

He later returned to pursue his writing ambitions in his native Skipton, which was not only the inspiration for Gunnarshaw, but also the location where the television drama *Cluff* was filmed.

THE BLINDNESS
OF SERGEANT
CLUFF

Gil North

GREAT NORTHERN

This edition published 2021 by
Great Northern Books
PO Box 1380, Bradford,
West Yorkshire, BD5 5FB

www.greatnorthernbooks.co.uk

© Gil North Limited 2021

Originally published in 1964 by Chapman & Hall Ltd

ISBN: 978-1-912101-40-5

Design by David Burrill

CIP Data
A catalogue for this book is available from the British Library

CHAPTER I

The heavy, measured tread approached nearer, passed the end of the back-street, and began to recede. It halted abruptly, the night more silent for the starting and stopping of sound, and then returned, louder but not so loud as before.

The man pressed against the cold stone of an outhouse wall stayed still, blending with the dark, the brim of his hat pulled well down, the collar of his macintosh turned up about his chin, hands hidden deep in his pockets.

A beam of light stabbed. He blinked, dazzled, and lifted a hand to shield his eyes. The blurred, bulky shape behind the torch expelled its breath in a long sigh.

"Put it out!" Detective-constable Barker ordered.

A sharp click plunged him into darkness again, blacker now. His sight recovered and adjusted gradually to bring the policeman into focus. A voice asked, "Any luck?" He didn't reply and the voice added, "He's never been seen in this part of the town."

"He was seen on the other side." Barker paused. "And almost caught."

The wind funnelled down the street behind him, blowing off the moors, cutting like a knife. He could sense the rain driving in tiny darts past his half-frozen cheeks. The seconds passed. He wasn't doing any good here and the policeman seemed reluctant to continue on his beat.

"And you?" Barker asked.

"Not a soul stirring. It's quiet as the grave."

Barker's feet felt like two blocks of ice. The rain, in his imagination at least, percolated through his clothing to his skin, its flow over his numbed limbs reinforced by the unpleasant trickles running down his neck.

"Caleb Cluff?" the policeman said.

"No point in two of us being in the same spot."

He lost track of how long it was since the policeman had left him. The luminous paint marking the figures on the face of his wristlet watch failed to function. Occasionally, in a quieter interval between gusts, he heard the chimes of the clock in the church tower, away over the roofs at the top of the High Street, but never for a sufficient period to count them accurately.

He stamped as he walked, the return of circulation physically painful, and beat his arms against his chest like flails, making himself smart. The bluffs of its terraced houses bounded the black, glistening river of Sevastopol Road and his pace slowed.

He stared up the narrow, cobbled slope between the backyards of Balaclava Street on one side and those of Inkerman Street on the other. The one-storey annexes at right-angles to the rows, part scullery, part W.C., part coal-place, separated the yards and hid the windows of the living-rooms. Here and there a yellow, oblong glow under the eaves showed a bedroom occupied behind drawn curtains. Far up the slope a shaft of brighter light speared the dark, directly over the gently-pitched roof of the outbuildings below it.

He started to run, the high-toned scream ringing in his ears. Doors opened: men shouted: women chattered excitedly. Something charged from one of the gates and butted him fairly in the midriff.

He snatched at air, toppling, trying frantically to regain his balance, and crashed to the cobbles. Farther off, in Sevastopol Road, a dog barked. Struggling to rise, shoes dug into his ribs, knocking him flat once more, driving the breath from his lungs. He tried again with no more success and this time he lay crushed under a squirming, wriggling weight that spouted threats and curses. Fingers clutched and he fought back to protect himself.

They dragged his attacker away and someone said, "It wasn't him." Neighbours hauled him to his feet and a woman brushed him down with her hands.

Speechless with anger, the man they'd pulled off Barker sobbed with rage and a confusion of voices made a cacophony of the night. A large figure, the light from the single gas-lamp falling on its stained Burberry and its shapeless tweed hat, helping itself along with a walking-stick, panting, accompanied by a limping dog, hurried towards the milling crowd. The people quietened and began to shiver in the cold. "It's all over," Sergeant Cluff told them. "Get back to your homes." They dispersed unwillingly in spite of their scantily clad bodies, leaving the Sergeant there and Barker, the man who'd fought with him and the dog.

"I missed him too," the Sergeant said. "Clive went after him but he used his boot. He was faster than either of us."

"I'd have killed him, Mr Cluff," the man stated, recovering his voice at last. "If I'd got my hands on him, I'd have killed him."

"Calm down, Jack."

"He was up there," and Jack pointed to the roof over the scullery.

"Tell us about it indoors."

The cloth of Barker's trousers clung stickily to one knee where he'd skinned it. In the lighted living-room he could see that Jack was young, in love, very serious. His wife, in a thick dressing-gown, as young as her husband, huddled over the embers of a dying fire, her feet bare. She held the edges of the gown together at her breasts with a hand on which the knuckles showed white, the tight material hinting at nakedness underneath. Clive nuzzled the detective-constable's leg and he bent down to examine the paw which the dog lifted appealingly, whimpering a little.

The Sergeant unbuttoned his coat. He leaned on his stick near the door from the scullery, frowning but breathing more easily. "Mary was having a bath," Jack said, standing close to his wife, who reached up and put her free hand into his.

"He wouldn't have harmed her."

"It isn't that. He was watching—"

"I hadn't anything on," his wife whispered, and confessed, "The curtains weren't drawn properly."

"It's clear glass," Jack interrupted. "It used to be a bedroom before I got it converted. I could have caught him if—" and he glared at Barker. "I was down here finishing the paper when Mary screamed. I heard the bump as he jumped down into the yard. It didn't take me a second to get after him."

"We'll have him," Cluff promised. "He'd a close shave tonight, closer than he's ever had. We shan't stop looking for him."

"His eyes!" and Mary shuddered.

"No one you knew?"

"His nose was flattened against the window. I was too frightened—"

"We haven't been married long," Jack said.

"You don't need to tell me that."

Jack disengaged his hand from his wife's and put his arm round her shoulders, her head against his hip: "We're going to have a baby—"

A blush spread over Mary's pale face: she buried it against her husband, refusing to meet their eyes.

The Sergeant gestured to Barker and turned for the door: "That's good news. She's safe with you."

CHAPTER II

The room was dark, except for a lighter shading where the curtains shut out the dawn. Mrs Mole said, "The children'll be up before us."

"I can't hear them moving." The Inspector swung his legs to the floor and sat for a moment on the edge of the bed before he crossed to the window and parted the curtains: "It's still raining."

They slept at the front. Over the roofs of the semi-detached houses opposite the pastures on the hill-sides showed dark and sodden, backgrounded by the higher moors, the road from which his own avenue branched an undulating ribbon, climbing the slopes, disappearing behind the crests and coming into view again. "It never does anything else in Gunnarshaw," Mole continued. "We ought to have webbed feet in this town." The road, leading as it did to the Sergeant's cottage, depressed him. "What with the weather," he said, "and Cluff—!"

A postman passed his gate as a man emerged from that belonging to the nearer of the two houses in the adjoining block. His neighbour, short, chunky, with rounded shoulders, unhealthily fat, eyes heavily pouched behind thin-rimmed spectacles, wore a workaday cloth cap, out of place in this district, and a woollen muffler under the collar of his macintosh.

"The post's early today," the Inspector remarked, watching the two men meet and stop and exchange a few words. The postman shook his head without troubling either to look in his bag or to go through the bundle of envelopes in his hand and continued along the pavement. "Nothing for us either," Mole said.

He had his socks and his trousers on and was buttoning his shirt when the doorbell rang, jerking Mrs Mole upright in bed. It didn't stop but shrilled continuously, without a pause, urgent, disturbing. He slipped his feet into his slippers and his arms into the old jacket he favoured for his morning chores. On the landing his schoolboy son poked his head out of his bedroom: "There's someone at the door," and he replied, irritated, "I'm not deaf."

He hurried down the stairs, across the small, square hall, and turned back the latch of the lock. "Good God!" he exclaimed. "What's happened?" Without stopping to put on his shoes or a raincoat he ran after his caller, past the garage built on to the house in line with the front door, round its corner, along the macadamed path into which the main drive narrowed. His own back door, set in the gable end, faced his nearest neighbour's across a shrubbery and a fence and an identical shrubbery on the other side.

The path continued by a large lawn to end finally at a hedge separating Mole's garden from one backing a house some distance away looking in the opposite direction to his. A gap in the privet witnessed where his visitor had forced a way through and the two of them made it larger. A hand that trembled slightly indicated the corner behind the hedge where a party fence like that shared by the Inspector joined it. Someone had dropped a bucket filled with ashes and cinders near a dustbin.

He said "Good God!" again, from his knees, looking up with a shocked expression at the headmaster of the Secondary Modern school. "In your garden!"

"Very nearly in yours," Rigsby pointed out, Mole's agitation calming his. "I was coming out to the bin." – and he wore slippers like the Inspector – "I could hardly believe my eyes. I didn't go back. I came straight through the hedge to you."

A woman appeared at the top of the garden, by the house to which it belonged. "Your wife," Mole said, scrambling to his feet.

"She doesn't know."

"Keep her away."

"Of course."

Mole dived through the hedge: "I'll get on the phone. If you'd make sure nobody interferes," and he ran as fast as he could for his own door.

Sergeant Cluff, up to this point on his normal course between his cottage and Gunnarshaw, walking at his usual speed, turned at the top of the hill where the first houses of the town began instead of continuing straight forward. Clive at his heels still limped slightly from last night's kick but wagged his tail at Barker, who waited by Mole's gate, outside which the police surgeon's car was already parked.

"Sergeant," Mrs Mole said from her kitchen doorway as they went down the garden path, and, "Leave the dog with me." He nodded absently and gave an automatic order to

Clive, whose head drooped. His eyes had wandered the short distance over the shrubbery and the fence to the closed door in the nearby gable. "He'd gone to work before we knew about it," the Inspector's wife explained.

"There's no one else in?"

She snapped a little; "It's only half-an-hour since."

The blocks of semi-detached houses, occasionally varied by a detached building, formed a square, facing outwards on to the avenues, two of which ran from the old coach road in and out of Gunnarshaw, itself the third side of the square, a fourth parallel to it connecting them. The area of gardens at their backs bounded by the houses was large and reasonably private, the hedges high, the fences solid, removed from the public gaze. They pushed through the gap at the far edge of Mole's lawn, making it wider still.

He hadn't been moved yet. Doctor Hamm was making his preliminary examination, stared at by Mole, in full uniform now, cap and greatcoat, the rain dulling his silver insignia and his buttons, less heavy than during the night, more of a mist than a downpour, and the wind had dropped. Rigsby walked along his path, keeping his eyes away from the body with which the day had greeted him, and told Cluff, "I shall have to be getting off to school."

The Sergeant nodded.

"My wife's upset," the headmaster added, a tall, athletic man, distinguished, greying at the temples. "You won't disturb her more than necessary?" He admitted, "It gave me quite a shock as well," and asked, "He's not the man you've been looking for, the Peeping Tom we've had about for the last six months?"

"You don't know him then?"

"I can't remember ever having seen him before. We weren't disturbed during the night." He glanced over his shoulder at the house next to his own: "My neighbours are away," and began to walk off. "You can see for yourself, nobody's been over my garden. With the ground so wet the tracks would have shown, both on the lawn and the flowerbeds." He waited a moment. "You know where to find me," and left.

"Hardly the place for this sort of thing," Doctor Hamm remarked, straightening, and grinned. "Amongst the town notables, teachers, doctors, solicitors, dentists, true-blue conservatives." He shot a quick glance at Mole. "And police officers."

The body looked clean in its corner, almost ready for the coffin, the edges of the tears in its clothing black not crimson, hardly darker than the soaked cloth between them, the depressed wound on the side of the head, above the left ear, washed by the rain.

"Sometime during the night," the surgeon said. "It's difficult to tell exactly in this sort of weather. I'll know more when I get him on the slab."

"Our bedroom looks on to the road," Mole interrupted, "but the children didn't hear anything either."

"Half a gale blowing. With so many trees it'd be noisy," and Cluff turned to Barker. "You'll have to make a search."

"For the weapon?"

"Two weapons."

"There's no doubt about the knife," Hamm said. "The other could have been anything heavy, stick, stone, iron bar, but rough and with a broad surface."

"I've got men on the way," Mole told them impatiently. "The photographer too." No congratulations were forthcoming and he shouted, "Just a minute! Where are you off to?"

"I'll be back," Cluff said, shaking his head at Barker and following the surgeon through the hedge.

They walked towards the Inspector's front gate. "You'll let me have him?" Hamm asked.

"Mole will, as soon as he's done what's necessary here. I'll see you later."

"Meantime?" the doctor said, his hand on the door of his car, and as Cluff made for the gate next to Mole's he added, "You might as well suspect the Inspector or Rigsby."

"These four houses are the nearest: the third's empty. This is the only one left where they might have noticed anything."

"They say she's young," Hamm remarked, offhandedly.

Cluff glanced at him sharply: "Bright Culter isn't."

"You take my meaning," the doctor replied, and climbed behind the steering wheel.

CHAPTER III

He opened the gate quietly and walked up the short drive to the front door, the windows of the house staring down at him blankly. Its woodwork, like the gutters and fall-pipes, had been recently painted, the stone walls up to the level of the pebble-dashing repointed not long ago. It was neat and well-kept, the property in good condition. He stretched out a hand to the bellpush and then lowered it without ringing.

He paused again by the back door in the gable, which was still closed, and continued along the path, following the line of the boundary fence, between the shrubbery and the lawn. The shrubbery ended at a small shed, separated from it by a patch of concrete, and he saw through its one window a rack of carpenter's tools and a workbench fitted with various attachments, a lathe, a vice, a grindstone. A rockery had been built on the other side of the shed, in the corner diagonal to that in which the body lay, the stones of various shapes and sizes but none of them small, those at the base firmly fixed by the weight above, the ones towards the top loose in the wet soil, which was so saturated that the water trickled over it. Mole looked at him over the hedge and said nothing: Barker was stooped by a flowerbed, poking fastidiously amongst withered leaves.

He turned, in plain view from Culter's house, especially

from the one large window of French type that almost filled the lower part of the wall facing the lawn. A fire burnt in the grate of the room inside, which was comfortably furnished if somewhat old-fashioned, its colourings dark, its appointments solid and heavy, but Mrs Culter had been very old herself and fixed in her ways. The lack of interest in his presence worried him.

A uniformed sergeant and four constables marched noisily along the path on Mole's side of the fence: a man with a tripod and a large, black case and flash bulb apparatus struggled from a car that had taken the place of Hamm's outside the Inspector's gate: an engine laboured up the hill from Gunnarshaw and an ambulance drew up behind the car. The Sergeant had a sense of movement, not in these nearer houses but in the houses farther away, of curtains fluttering and eyes watching, of a mounting excitement as the situation developed.

He went back to the side door and knocked, but almost inaudibly, hardly waiting before he turned its knob. It opened at his touch and he stepped into a small enclosed vestibule with a coalplace on one side and from there, through a second door, into a kitchen. A fire burnt in the grate here too: crockery and the remains of breakfast occupied a table: a tap dripped slowly, drop by drop, into a porcelain sink: an electric kettle with its plug lying beside it stood on the hotplate of an electric oven.

He considered the room, letting his eyes rove. A smudge of red on the tip of a cigarette stubbed in a saucer matched a red smear on the rim of the cup beside whose base it lay. A packet of cigarettes spewed its contents on the mantelpiece and he knew the man whose vests and underpants and shirts aired on a rack hoisted to the ceiling didn't smoke. He noticed details here and there that didn't fulfil the promise of the house's exterior, a film of dust on the dresser shelves, blobs of fat spattered from a frying pan on the oven top, a tidemark round the sink, grease in the furrows of the draining board attached to it, dried mud on the coconut matting in front of an armchair containing a cushion whose cover was beginning to gape.

His ears pricked. A door to a front passage stood ajar and he went through it, past the panelling enclosing a flight of stairs to their foot, where the passage expanded into a hall. The sounds were louder, more apparent over the steady flow of running water draining into an outlet pipe, someone retching and vomiting.

He retreated to the kitchen but not out-of-doors again. He clenched his fist and battered loudly on the panel of the inner door, waiting just inside with his hat in his hand and the handle of his walking-stick crooked over his arm. His Burberry ballooned over the swelling mound of his belly and the thick, rough tweed of his shapeless trousers' legs had a faint scent of the open air.

"I couldn't make anyone hear," he explained to the woman who advanced towards him from the passage. "The door wasn't locked."

Sweat filmed her forehead thinly and her bout of sickness had whitened her cheeks, the scarlet of her lips vivid by contrast. "Who are you?" she asked, her voice unsteady.

"A police sergeant," and he introduced himself. She swayed on her feet and clutched at the back of an upright chair. "You're not well," he said, half in statement, half in question.

"I'm all right."

The heat of the kitchen made his face, already flayed by his walk from the cottage, shine redder. He loosened his coat, puffing slightly, and sat down, contemplating for a while the toes of his brown, grained-leather boots, before looking up at her, smiling: "I'm making enquiries." He shrugged, dismissing the matter as of small importance. "Whether anyone was wakened during the night, an unusual noise, people talking—"

"Mr Culter isn't in."

"Naturally not. You sleep here too?"

"I work here."

"Don't judge the town by what's been happening recently, a man lurking outside, peeping in through the windows, listening to private conversations."

"That's what you've come about?"

"You don't look well at all. Why don't you take a chair?"

"I didn't hear anything, not last night, nor any night."

She wore an inexpensive, flowered dress and he put her down as in her late twenties, though the hardness of her eyes bespoke a whole lifetime of experience. Her face was innocent of makeup apart from her lipstick but her pores were enlarged, stippling her skin, and clogged near the bases of her nostrils. Her body had lost the firmness of youth, the skin under her jaws slack, loose at the roots of her neck.

"I shouldn't have disturbed you," he apologized.

Something about her made him believe that if he made advances she wouldn't repel them and she didn't strike him as virgin, or monogamous, but she wasn't old enough yet to have put sex behind her. "It's a large house," he added, "for one woman to run."

"I can manage."

Her voice had a coarseness in it, a timbre that jarred on his hearing, but a man didn't choose a woman for her speech if she was compliant in other ways. He said, "It always surprised me how Bright did," but she wasn't to be drawn. He went on, as much to himself as to her, "I remember when he was at school, not mine – we went to different ones – but we knew each other."

Her eyes narrowed and the colour had come back to her face. "You must have heard," he said. "After his mother was bedridden Bright did everything. She wouldn't have a nurse: he cooked for her and cleaned. It went on for a long time. She was in her eighties."

The woman, not tall but no shorter than the man lying dead out there behind the hedge that marked the boundary of Mole's garden, still maintained her silence. Little by little a notion grew in his mind of what she might really be. Her chin jutted, sharp, with a stubbornness about it, or a strength of will: her nose had a beak-like quality, predatory. She made him think of mean city streets, tucked away in the slums, of women at windblown corners, under the light of street-lamps, short macintoshes tightly belted about their waists, viciously intent in the rain on men who were strangers to them. He could find nothing in her common to the girls of Gunnarshaw, fresh and vital, smooth-skinned, complexions of peaches and cream, human but decently so, like Mary last night in Balaclava Street.

"Bright had to toe the line," he said. "It's wrong to speak ill of the dead but she was a tyrant of the first order." The woman moved to the door and held it open before he could gain his feet.

When he got outside the photographer he'd seen unpacking his gear was stowing it away in his car again and a small procession walked mutely down Mole's path on the other side of the fence, past Mrs Mole in her doorway, with Clive standing beside her, two ambulance attendants carrying between them a sheeted form on a stretcher, the Inspector and Barker bringing up the rear. He heard the woman gasp but he didn't look round. He felt her watching, as he watched, the stretcher slipped into position through the back doors of the ambulance, both attendants going round to its cab. "If you remember anything," he said, "anything, however small, you'll let me know?"

"There's nothing to remember," she told him, and turned into the house, closing the door.

Inspector Mole was unlocking his garage.

CHAPTER IV

They were crowded in Mole's car, Barker and Clive in the back, the Sergeant overflowing the passenger seat next to the Inspector, but it wasn't far to the mortuary, a small building hidden away behind the depot of the Council's Highways Department.

They left Clive in the anteroom and it seemed to Cluff that he came here too often. The only thing different was the body, stripped and extended on the central table, its skin white and a little wrinkled as if it had actually been immersed in water. Doctor Hamm, in his stained white overall coat and his pink rubber gloves, waited for them, a scalpel in his hand. "Give me time," he said. "I went home for some breakfast."

A pile of clothing lay on a side-table. Inspector Mole examined it item by item, emptying the pockets as he did so, the scowl on his face growing. "Not even a tailor's label," he said, disgustedly. "Cheap, ready-made stuff, the shoes no better than cardboard, sold in a hundred multiple shops." He waved at the heap of personal possessions, dismissing them, a few currency notes, odd coins, cigarettes in a packet, matches, soiled handkerchief, a broken-toothed comb, a nail file, but no papers, no letters, nothing in writing that might have provided an identification.

The ribs of the corpse almost burst the skin under its

hollow, hairless chest and it was weedy and undersized, its belly concave, its arms and legs like matchsticks. The pinched face, imprinted with low cunning, gave no indication of what purpose this man had served in society or any hint that society had been deprived by his loss.

"Whoever got rid of him," Hamm commented, "probably did a public service. It's a pity you can't let well alone. The world would be a better place if men like that were drowned at birth." He lifted a dead hand and let it drop again. "He never did a day's work in his life. They're soft as putty. He's never walked when he could ride. The only air he's ever breathed has been in pubs and billiard halls and whores' bedrooms. I'll bet a pound to a penny when I open him up he's tubercular. I don't doubt he's had worse diseases than that." He jerked the head carelessly to one side so that his audience had a plainer view of the wound above the ear. "For what it's worth his skull's abnormally thin. He's a rat who wouldn't fight when he could run or he wouldn't have survived as long as he did. One good blow would do for him."

"A woman?" the Sergeant asked.

"A child, if it was in a temper."

"How much does he weigh?"

"What would you say – about eight stones? Not much more."

The Inspector had a feeling that he was being left out of things: "Does that matter? He wasn't knifed because he was under-weight."

"He needn't have been knifed at all," the doctor said. "That's obvious, surely. He didn't bleed much – those punctures are clean as a whistle, an unnecessary refinement."

He asked, "You've found it?"

"We'll go on looking."

"What makes you think you'll be successful? An infant would know enough, if it wanted to get rid of the knife, not to leave it lying about at the scene of the crime."

Cluff looked at the neat holes: "They're small."

"And deep. A stiletto, thin and pointed, needle-like." The doctor motioned with his scalpel. "You're holding me up. Now that you've discovered there's no short cut let me get on with it. You'll have to go the long way round if you're interested in finding out who he is."

The Sergeant walked away, collecting Clive in the anteroom, into the open air, and by the time Mole and Barker got outside he was passing the tar-boilers and the piles of gravel.

"Sergeant!" the detective-constable called, but Cluff's pace only quickened. The Inspector growled and offered his companion a lift.

"Where to?" Barker asked.

"Look here, this isn't a joke. You don't imagine anyone's going to let it drop?" Mole's tones expressed determination and emphasis. "He was in Rigsby's garden: he might have been in mine." He gripped the detective's arm. "Everybody who matters in the town lives up there."

"Bright Culter too?"

"I'm not including him." The Inspector looked thoughtful and then pulled himself together. "It's a reflection on us all."

"From what Hamm said he wouldn't have come to Gunnarshaw on his flat feet."

"The first thing's the photograph," and Mole opened the

door of his car. "It should be ready by now. You'd better do something about it if Cluff won't."

"I don't know—"

"I do. Get in!"

Barker did so reluctantly: "The Sergeant said nothing about—"

The Inspector interrupted him before he could finish the sentence. "He can't very well do without your help – or mine. This isn't someone he's acquainted with. It's not so easy for him this time."

"Perhaps he's got an idea."

"If it had happened anywhere else in the town I'd let him stew in his own juice but my reputation's at stake too." The Inspector couldn't get over it. "Practically on my own doorstep. If he won't take action, I will."

"He's got other things on his mind."

"That Peeping Tom? If it takes as long to bring this murderer to book as he's taking to catch that chap we'll all be in our graves without being any the wiser."

"He wasn't far off last night."

"Wasn't he? As things turned out you'd both have been better employed in my part of Gunnarshaw. The trouble with the C.I.D. is, they're never on the spot when they're wanted."

CHAPTER V

Cluff walked up the avenue past Mole's house, eyeing a little group of housewives, with shopping baskets to explain their presence, talking near the gate. The uniformed sergeant and his men were still visible between the Inspector's and Culter's but from the look of them they'd decided there wasn't much profit in further search for the missing knife. They lounged against the fence, contemplating the gardens gloomily, killing time until someone gave them orders to knock off duty, convinced they'd done all that could be expected of them.

The voices of the women lowered as Cluff went by and he showed no enthusiasm for them, unattracted. They came from the houses round about, smartly dressed, idle, their charwomen busy in their absences, and on an ordinary morning, if they'd had shopping to do, they'd have used their cars. Probably they thought as little of him as he did of them and he neither offered much of an advertisement for the efficiency of the police force nor improved the tone of the district. "I'd know where to look," one of them said after he'd gone by, loudly enough for him to hear, and he knew what she meant.

He ignored the countryside as he descended the hill beyond the last of the houses and climbed its successor and it wasn't so much his suspect who troubled him as the effect of an arrest on people left free. Clive trotted sedately and raindrops lay on the hawthorns. He hoped he was wrong and he'd no proof one way or the other but he couldn't see how there could be an alternative answer. He found no comfort in consoling himself that his actions might, in the end, be for a friend's good and the satisfaction of doing his duty wasn't much of a reward if it brought as well the dislike of people he'd known all his life. He arrived at the cottage without realizing how he'd got there and hung his hat and coat on the pegs in the passage after putting his stick in the corner by the front door.

Annie Croft looked up in surprise as he entered the living-room, the handle of a sweeper in her hand, the furniture piled back against the walls. She scowled and complained, "You should have stopped in Gunnarshaw."

"I don't have to give notice to come into my own house?"

He rescued his pipe and tobacco from the mantelpiece and retreated to the kitchen with his dog. His cat, Jenet, sat unhappily on the threshold of the open door, staring disdainfully at the rain, and he joined her there, bending to stroke her, but she turned deliberately away, wanting no truck with him, blaming him for Annie's activities. He leaned against the jamb, smoking, looking at the bare trees in his orchard and at his green-painted hen-hut, beyond them across the winter-dark pastures to the cloud-shrouded moors. It occurred to him after a while to root in the boot cupboard under the sink and he dragged out a collection of old local weekly newspapers. Kneeling on the floor, he started going through the "Situations Vacant" columns on the back pages.

"What do you want, rheumatism?" Annie demanded, from the passage doorway, and added ungraciously, "I haven't given it half a doing-over but it's not my fault. Get in there if you want to." The cat had already slipped past her into the living-room.

He climbed to his feet with one of the papers in his hand and she walked forward towards him: "Haven't you anything better to read?"

He pointed a finger at the item that had interested him: "What's her name?"

She screwed up her eyes to read the print.

"Bright didn't have to put an advert in the paper," Cluff said. "Plenty of people could have put him on to a housekeeper. He'd only to ask."

"You for instance?"

"What was she doing in Gunnarshaw anyway?"

"Won't she tell you?"

"You don't miss anything that's going on."

Annie's feathers ruffled a little: "Hilda Smith."

Cluff muttered, "I suppose it could be."

"It wouldn't take much making up either."

"What are they saying?" the Sergeant asked.

"I've got my uses, have I?"

"There's some subjects women don't talk to me about."

"Maybe men put it plainer."

"They might have done if I'd wanted to hear it from them. I didn't."

"Why the change then?"

"I was talking to her this morning."

"So she's got herself into trouble? It won't surprise anybody."

"It might surprise Bright Culter."

"He wants analysing," Annie asserted, "or she wouldn't be

working for him."

"He doesn't have to take other people's orders."

"His neighbours weren't fond of him as it was. He's given them cause to talk now."

"Maybe he wants to marry her. It's happened before."

"She knew that when she persuaded him to take her on."

"He must have been willing," Cluff pointed out.

"After fifty years, or nearly so, of his mother, he'd be willing for anything," and Annie put her arms akimbo. "What's he been up to?"

"Nothing."

"Her, then?"

"You don't sound worried."

"From Bright's point of view it couldn't be better. It'll need a shock to open his eyes."

"You've been studying her life history?"

"It's written all over her."

"Where does she come from?"

"You're the detective."

He said slowly, "If he's fond of her—" and stopped before he went on, "She'd be about the first thing he's ever had for himself."

"You get along well enough on your own. Why shouldn't he?"

The Sergeant threw the paper down: "She hasn't been there long."

"She hasn't had to be," Annie replied, meaningly. "He's a baby where women are concerned."

He said, from the passage doorway, "A pity he couldn't have someone like you working for him: he'd have learned his lesson," and went into the living-room. He lifted Jenet from the seat of his chair and sat down with the cat on his knees. Clive's limbs, on the rug, twitched gently and the clock ticked. Subdued noises from the kitchen bore witness to Annie Croft's energy.

His eyes closed but he didn't go properly to sleep, halfway between sleeping and waking, making a vaguely conscious effort to stay there.

The next thing he heard was Annie slapping pots on the table. He said, "It's time you were off."

"I would have been if you hadn't turned up. Now you're here you'll want feeding."

"Never mind."

"I've cooked it. You'll get it down you if it chokes you."

About halfway through the afternoon, when he'd been alone in the cottage for some time, he looked at his watch. He waited until it started to get dark and, after he'd put the cat back in the chair, he made up the fire. The telephone in the passage rang and he let it ring until it stopped, not troubling to answer it. In the end he nodded at Clive, alert and on his feet, and took the dog with him when he collected his hat and Burberry and stick.

He didn't go directly down the hill into Gunnarshaw, any more than he'd come that way in the morning, branching instead past Mole's house and Culter's. So far as he could see everything that had taken place earlier in the day might not have happened at all. The avenue was its old peaceful self and if murder worried the residents hereabouts they'd decided not to show it, or perhaps they believed that by ignoring the more unpleasant facts of life they didn't exist. The doors of Mole's garage gaped but it was empty.

The Sergeant walked on, round this corner and that, through the outskirts of the town, not much of it level, down a hill, across a main road, up another steep slope between rows of houses that stopped at its crest. The land on the other side descended to a canal, its purpose as a park more apparent in its title than in its appointments. A few wooden seats nudged a railing at its upper boundary, dividing it from a copse, and grass innocent of amenities led down to a stretch of flatter ground provided with swings and a children's roundabout and a slide this side of a gravel path joining a swing bridge over the canal, which curved in a bow with its bulge against the base of the hill. A large mill extended for some distance along the towpath to which the bridge gave access, poking its chimney at the sky. Over the lower houses which began where the mill ended Cluff had a view of railway tracks and the buildings of a station.

He sat down on one of the seats, no children on the playground, and it was practically dark under the trees though the mill windows blazed with light, reflected in the still water. Cars and lorries, and an occasional bus, drove along the road in front of the railway station.

A buzz shrieked and he checked the time on his half-hunter. In the distance a murmur of voices and the beat of feet on stone flags mingled with the noise of the passing traffic. People began to climb the slope towards him in twos and threes, not many of them, and they didn't notice him in the shadows. He craned forward on the seat, recognizing them more by their shapes than by their blurred faces, and the field emptied but he stayed where he was.

"Bright," he called softly.

The solitary figure froze and for a few more moments Cluff didn't stir. The movements of the man's head showed how he was trying to trace the origin of the summons and a tenseness about him made the Sergeant think he was going to take to his heels.

"It's me," Cluff said, advancing slowly, and there was no lessening of tension in the man he approached. "Your housekeeper told you at dinnertime?" he asked.

"You shouldn't have bothered her."

"I had to. You know why."

"Everybody does by this time."

"He was found just over your back hedge."

"The Inspector's too. And in Rigsby's garden."

"It beats me," Cluff said, "why you go on living there."

"I've as much right to as anybody else."

"That's about the only reason your mother had when she moved into that house."

"She could have bought them all up and still have had as much again to spare."

"So can you – you got it all."

"I'm entitled to it."

"But you're still working at the mill."

"You've put your finger on it," Culter said, bitterly. "I'm not good enough for the neighbours."

"Your mother enjoyed seeing them squirm. You don't."

"They can't get rid of me that easy."

"It's no use asking you if you heard anything in the night?"

"No."

"Where do you sleep?"

"The back."

"And her?"

"The front."

"I'll walk over the hill with you," Cluff said.

They reached the streets and the lamp-standards, Culter no taller than the Sergeant's shoulder, and was it Cluff's imagination, or did he stoop more than usual, his shoulders rounder? His feet dragged and his fat quivered: the artificial light heightened his pallor and his eyes were dull behind the lenses of his glasses.

"Bright—" Cluff said again, but he didn't know how to go on, afraid to create a barrier between them he wouldn't be able to breach later, however much he wanted to help. He sought for words as they descended to the main road and managed finally, "People aren't always what they seem to be."

"Were you waiting for me to tell me that?"

The Sergeant stopped: "Just that."

"I'm old enough to make my own judgments."

"It's a small town," Cluff said. "I doubt if I've realized how small it is until today. Maybe the way we live doesn't fit us to cope with strangers."

"Live!"

"They all respect you. You stood by your mother to the end."

"I'm older than you are," and was there a sneer in Culter's voice?

"Only by a year or two."

"You didn't have to live in the same house with her."

"You'd your job."

"I had to give that up for the last six months."

"You've gone back to it."

"It's all I know," and Culter crossed the road without looking either way, starting up the opposite hill, which would take him home.

The Sergeant took a step or two after him, suddenly aware of Clive, not remembering the dog in the park or since. The angry hoot of a car horn startled him and drove him back to the kerb.

He followed the road towards the centre of the town and he hadn't got far before he came on Mole's car parked outside a newsagent's and tobacconist's. He walked faster but not fast enough and before he could get past the shop the door opened and the Inspector stepped on to the pavement. He had an envelope in his hand and Cluff couldn't avoid him nor he Cluff. "Caleb," he said, and slid a photograph half-out of the envelope, glancing down at the face of the dead man. "I've been in all the shops in this part of the town. No one'll admit ever having seen him." He crossed to his car: "You're going to the station?"

"Who said so?"

"You've seen the evening papers? They've got the whole story. I'm in it too. I don't like jokes about murder being served to the police on a platter."

"They'll get tired of it."

"Barker's contacted you?"

Cluff shook his head.

"I told him to get back by teatime." Mole paused. "He might have had better luck than I've had."

"Someone's going to get hurt," the Sergeant said.

"Whoever the murderer is he ought to have thought of that."

"Not the guilty, the innocent—"

"Hold on!" Mole exclaimed suspiciously. "What have you been doing with your time?"

"Hadn't you guessed? I've been at home all day," but the Sergeant walked to the car as well. He opened its door and gestured Clive inside.

CHAPTER VI

Barker leaned on the counter in the outer office, talking to the Duty Constable. Mole came into the station first, with Cluff and Clive following. The Inspector looked at Barker and then round at Cluff, and back at Barker again. The constable scratched the end of his nose.

"I tried to ring you," Barker told the Sergeant. "I couldn't get a reply." He went on, "He wasn't staying at any of the lodging houses I've been to. It wasn't worth trying the hotels: they'd hardly have let him in."

"You didn't leave it there?" Mole protested.

"I asked at the bus station."

"You'd a photograph too."

"It made no difference."

"And the trains?"

"They don't remember either. A lot of people go off for the half-day when it's early closing, as it was yesterday."

"If some of those collectors talked less to their friends they'd see more," Mole said, and went to the door of the C.I.D. room. He opened it and walked inside.

"He's taking over your branch, Caleb?" the Duty Constable asked.

"They're his neighbours: he has to live with them. And they're important."

"Who to?" the Duty Constable wanted to know.

The Inspector was looking at a package on Cluff's blotting pad when the Sergeant entered. He said, "It's all you can do," and glanced at Barker, who had come into the room as well. "There's another photograph here, and his fingerprints. It's not beyond the bounds of possibility he'd a record." He pushed a sheet of paper into view. "I've had it typed for you, Caleb. Patterson at Headquarters knows already."

"How?"

"He's in charge of the County C.I.D., isn't he? Someone mentioned it to him on the phone."

"You?"

"Not me – it's not a matter for the uniformed force. Rigsby perhaps," and the Inspector looked for a pen on the table that Cluff used as a desk. Failing to find one, he unscrewed the top of his own fountain pen and offered it to the Sergeant: "I've got a police car standing by at the back: they'll be at Headquarters in an hour and a half." He waited a moment. "We're getting nowhere in Gunnarshaw. The Chief Superintendent'll expect it from you. He'll circulate the photograph and the details for us."

Cluff didn't move.

"It's not how," Mole persisted. "It's not so much even who—"

"You've got an idea about that?"

"It's why," Mole continued. "Once we know who he is it'll be clearer. Somebody had a reason for getting rid of him."

"You don't need my signature," Cluff said. "You could have signed this letter for me, or written in your own name."

"Haven't I just told you, the C.I.D. isn't my pigeon."

"You can have it so far as I'm concerned."

"What's the matter with you this time? You haven't got an eye on one of your friends already?"

"Not in the way you mean."

"I'd forgotten. They aren't capable of breaking the law."

The Sergeant put his name to the letter: "You can do what you like with it," and he stalked out of the room while Mole sealed the package. Barker hesitated before following and arrived in the outer office to see the street door closing.

The Duty Constable said, "Go after him: he's on to something." He winked. "It won't be what the Inspector thinks either. It never is."

Clive looked round as Barker caught them up and Cluff objected, "You've been on your feet all day."

"I'm not tired." He fell into step with the Sergeant. "Hamm rang through. There's nothing he hasn't told us already except that the killing took place about eleven and before midnight." The detective-constable sounded disappointed. "I'd hoped—"

"What?"

"That man we were after in Little Crimea."

"He couldn't have been in two places at the same time."

"It wouldn't have fitted. There's nothing to connect them anyway."

They walked in silence, across the High Street at its bottom end, on past the mill. A diesel train hooted mournfully and the buffers of waggons clashed in a shunting yard. Hadn't he told them already, Barker thought, that he'd been here? He considered repeating himself and decided against it.

He stayed with Clive in the arch of the draughty tunnel that led from the railway station approach, through an entrance blocked by an iron grille, on to the main platform while Cluff turned into the booking hall. The Sergeant walked past the two pigeon-holes in the wooden and glass screen on his left and through a door beyond them into the ticket office. A Scottish express, white destination boards a blur, windows a continuous unbroken line of light, raced through the station shrieking at the signal box on the north side, wheels beating a rhythmic tattoo. Barker put a hand down to stroke the dog's head, murmuring encouragement, and the sound of the train died away in the distance. The station lamps still used gas and he could understand why the railways were losing money, no one at the barrier, not a porter in sight, grime thick on the walls, paint old and flaking, the travel posters tattered and scrawled over with crude, pencilled humour.

Cluff came back, his tread resounding on the wooden floor of the booking hall, sharper as he stepped into the stone-flagged tunnel. He stared at a trolley with rusted iron wheels, the planks of its board platform rotting: "I thought there might still be a chance: they haven't got rid of yesterday's tickets," and he set off for the town.

Barker's eyebrows lifted: "There must be a couple of dozen and more. We don't know who used them."

"Only one outward return from Liverpool."

"Liverpool?"

"It's not long since I was there.* More than coincidence: I've often noticed it – one case links with another."

"Whoever travelled with it could have gone back."

"I doubt it."

"He'd nothing to show where he came from," Barker

* _More Deaths for Sergeant Cluff_

objected, remembering the dead man's possessions in the mortuary, "no half ticket if the other portion you've seen was his."

"It could have been taken from his pockets: it would have to be." He looked at Barker. "They can't hide their origin. It's their accent. You can tell a Merseysider anywhere."

"But you never heard him speak."

The iron-railed pens of an auction mart, faintly aromatic of sheep tridlings, loomed over the wall they were passing and ahead, at the opposite corner of a road junction, the windows of a workmen's cafe were still lit. "If he did come yesterday it couldn't have been for the first time," Cluff said. "He either knew where to go in Gunnarshaw or he met someone who took him round." The ferrule of his stick poked at a crack in the flags. "You can't always get a bite to eat on the station. The buffet was closed altogether a few weeks back. It's hardly worth anybody's trouble to run."

The cafe was long and narrow, its door at the corner, its one room running parallel with the side-street. A round-bellied vinegar bottle stoppered with a brown-threaded porcelain shaker, a tin salt cellar and pepper pot, bottles of brown sauce and tomato, occupied the centre of a dingy white cloth on each of a line of tables under the windows. A long counter ran down the opposite side, tea-urn at one end, sugar bowl nearby, and a teaspoon tied to a string fixed to the wood somewhere out of sight. Apart from the Sergeant and Barker there weren't any customers.

The proprietor behind the counter nodded and said, "I was just thinking of shutting up shop." He frowned, "It was all right before they started a canteen at the mill," and grinned wryly. "I'd about as well not bother to open up again." Cluff glanced at the urn and the man took a couple of cups from the shelves behind him and filled them with strong, almost black, tea. He pushed them and the sugar bowl and a milk jug he rescued from under the counter across its top.

The Sergeant said, "I don't know why they don't come in any more. It's the only place in town you can get a decent cup of tea." Barker sipped and wrinkled his nose. He reached for the milk jug again to dilute the tannin and thought of letting go the spoon to see whether it would stand up in the brew without assistance.

"Owt to eat?" their host asked, a big, tremendously stomached man, in his shirt sleeves, with the shirt neck open and lacking a collar. "Give yourself a treat," he pleaded, and extracted two pork pies from under a glass dome. "If I keep them much longer they'll get away on me." He started to break a third into pieces and dropped its fragments over the counter to Clive. "If it doesn't poison the dog you'll survive."

"They're nearly as good as Annie's," the Sergeant said, munching.

"She's spoilt you."

"Trade that bad, Fred?"

"There isn't any."

"People must be daft. If ever a man was an advertisement for his own wares, you are."

"I ought to be. I have to eat them."

"I used to come in here for my dinners," Cluff said, "when I was at school. They didn't have school meals then. It was too far to go back to Cluff's Head farm even if there'd been more than two buses a day."

"Did they have buses?" Fred said. "I thought it'd be stage coaches when you were a lad."

"A plate of meat and potato pie for fourpence," Cluff mused. "Sixpence if you wanted a double helping. Apple dumpling and white sauce for threepence. I'd nothing else day in and day out for six years. The dearest thing was a cup of tea – they charged you a penny."

"It set you up for life."

"I'll have another pie," Cluff said, "and so will Barker."

"By gum, I'll be showing a profit."

"Not if you go on feeding the dog."

"Aye, I didn't think you'd be forking out for him."

"They stop here off the trains?" the Sergeant asked.

"Once in a blue moon. Who goes on a train these days anyhow?"

"Sometimes then?"

"One in a hundred," and Fred's expression was shrewd. "Come on, you're not in here because you're sorry for me."

"You've still got it?" Cluff asked Barker, who failed for a moment to understand what he meant and then dug in his inside jacket pocket for the photograph he'd carried about most of the day. Fred looked at it with his head on one side: "I saw you going past earlier on. I half expected you in then," he told the detective-constable, who flushed and studied the floor at his feet. "Once," the café proprietor said. "Maybe a couple of weeks back."

"Not yesterday?"

"No fear."

"A Liverpudlian?"

"You couldn't mistake it." Fred's stubby finger, its lower

joint furred with grey, wiry hairs, poked at the picture. "That's who was done in, eh?"

"I didn't say."

"You didn't need to. He couldn't have chosen a better place to get himself killed. They'd do with their noses rubbing in the dirt, some of that lot up there on the hill."

"Bright Culter as well?"

"Bright wants a bomb under him. He's wanted it for years."

"Doesn't he ever come in? He lived upstairs long enough."

"If his mother had had any sense he'd be up there yet."

"She made plenty out of this place."

"I paid her plenty for it. And she'd shops at every street corner down past the mill. People used to cough up in those days." He shook his head. "The only time she ever spent a penny herself was when she bought that house."

"She'd come up the hard way," Cluff said. "She could move if she wanted."

"It didn't make Bright a gentleman."

"She didn't want him to be. She liked the neighbours to see him coming home from the mill."

"By!" Fred said, remembering. "She could be an awkward devil when she wanted. She didn't care a jot for anyone."

The Sergeant picked up the photograph and stowed it in a pocket. "He didn't happen to say much?"

"He asked his way."

"To where we found him this morning?"

"Thereabouts."

"No names?"

"Too foxy for that. I'd as leave not have had him in at all."

"And you couldn't get it out of him?"

"Not for want of trying. I'd have been in touch with you, Caleb, but no one told me it was him."

The Sergeant put some coins on the counter and took his change. Fred said, "Nobody's ever offered me a tip in my life."

"We wouldn't insult you," Cluff replied, and started for the door after draining his cup.

CHAPTER VII

The Sergeant kept silent as they made their way to the High Street. Both Barker and the dog expected him to call it a day and set off round the corner by the church to his cottage. It wasn't late yet, only a little past seven and, while the pavements weren't by any means crowded, a number of people went backwards and forwards past them as they stood on the kerb by the skeletons of the stalls, their canvas roofs and looser parts stored away for the night in old stables down the ginnels, which occupied the setts between it and the carriageway. Youths and girls making for Further Education classes glanced at them before turning into the double doors of the Institute next to the Public Library. Older people, on their way to the pictures or for a drink in one of the public houses, slowed and mumbled a greeting to Cluff, hesitating, hoping that he'd give them an opening for a lengthier conversation, but he didn't do more than nod in answer. Barker felt that his face was deliberately stern and forbidding and they got tired, and annoyed, and went about their business, grumbling at the Sergeant's closeness.

It was cold waiting there, for nothing, so far as the young detective could see, in particular, and he hadn't had much sleep the night before. He wasn't quite sure whether he wanted to go back to his lodgings and to bed, or not. They didn't seem to be serving any useful purpose in the High Street but he'd never been able to distinguish between relevance or the lack of it in anything the Sergeant did. He decided that, on the whole, it was safest to assume they weren't here by accident but he wished the weather would improve. The prickings of conscience troubled him. If Cluff hadn't blamed him he blamed himself and, if he'd been on his toes and the thought had occurred to him, he could just as easily have found out about the tickets at the station, or called at Fred's café, as the Sergeant. Or could he? He glanced sideways at his superior and until the café proprietor they'd neither of them discovered anyone who'd admitted to conversation with last night's victim. He'd have been able to understand the object of Cluff's visit to the ticket office better if they'd called at the café first: as it was, how had the Sergeant known that their inquiries concerned a man from Merseyside?

Across the road a few cars were drawing up outside the Town Hall. Their drivers, one of whom was Rigsby, met other men approaching on foot and climbed with them the broad steps to the entrance. Cluff shifted his weight and said, "Has it ever occurred to you? Except for the headmaster and one or two others they're all small people." Barker counted heads to confirm the statement and the Sergeant went on, "Somebody ought to write a thesis on the relationship between height and so-called public service. It's compulsive – they're driven to interfere with what doesn't concern them by their own physical insignificance and shortness of stature. You or me, we'd be afraid of making exhibitions of ourselves but small people aren't sensitive, not outwardly, just belligerent," – and he considered before he concluded – "unless the stuffing's knocked out of them by someone more determined than they are."

He would have made two of most of the men vanishing importantly into the Town Hall and still have had something to spare. "It didn't use to matter," he said. "Years ago the gentry served without any thought of reward, either financial or in self-importance, but democracy's let the little men in. They get their allowances and time off from the jobs for which they draw their wages and what have they got in their heads – or where did they learn it – that qualifies them to run our lives for us?"

The traffic – mostly cars: the lorries had stopped passing some time ago – thinned to a trickle and then into nothing, long periods going by without anything at all driving along the road. The pedestrians too had gone, to their various pleasures, and the street, except for an hour or so between half past nine and half past ten when people returned in their opposite directions, would be empty for the rest of the night. There wasn't a lot of difference, Barker thought, between here and Sevastopol Road.

"Have you read Bacon?" Cluff demanded.

"He won't try anything tonight," Barker replied, irrelevantly, his mind busy with another subject altogether, thinking of the Peeping Tom.

"On 'Deformity'," the Sergeant added.

"He's a fool if he does," Barker said, "unless he thinks this other business will keep us busy. But no, he wouldn't."

"He won't try anything," Cluff agreed, collecting his thoughts. "You're quite right." The church clock struck eight. "We'll take a walk. It's warmer than standing still."

"To the office?"

"Have you seen the Inspector going home?"

They took yet another road, where the lights in the foyer of the town's one remaining cinema lit up a dry patch of pavement protected from the rain by a glass canopy jutting from the façade. On either side of the entrance steps painted cowboys rode and shot on large posters. The Sergeant turned in and stopped to gaze at the stills displayed in a show-case. "You've seen it?" he asked Barker.

"I haven't had the chance."

"I enjoy them too," Cluff said. "They're the only kind I'd come to see, on a Saturday afternoon, with children in the front rows—"

He pushed at the bar on the glass doors and Barker and Clive trailed him into the inner hall. "What are you going to do with the dog?" Barker said, not that he'd put it past Cluff to take Clive inside with him if he wanted to.

The manager, Gunnarshaw or no Gunnarshaw in a dinner suit, black tie and all, leaned against the box-office, flanked by a sweet counter whose attendant chatted to a girl in a white overall with a tray containing ice-cream and cartons of soft drinks slung round her neck. "Sergeant," he said, not very cheerfully, and looked at Clive. "I'll let anything in that pays. I'm losing money, not making it."

"You're not the first man who's told me that tonight."

"It's good to know there's someone in the same boat."

"I thought they liked this sort of film in Gunnarshaw."

"When they can sit at home and watch something similar on television?"

"I couldn't: I don't have one. You've got your regulars."

"I'd have to be in your job to trace them."

"For Westerns anyway."

"One or two," the manager admitted.

"Like Bright Culter?"

"He comes to see the cowboys. It's a terrible business that, Mr Cluff."

"Not in Bright's garden. You'll be seeing him sometime during the week. He won't miss this."

"He was here last night."

"By himself?"

"What do you think?"

"He's got a housekeeper now."

"He'd know about it if he started taking her about in this town."

"We're all kids at heart," Cluff said. "We can't live like those people on the screen but we'd have enjoyed it if we could."

"Between you and me, nobody ever lived like it."

"It doesn't matter so long as we think so. What time do you finish?"

"It's a long show – a couple of features. A quarter to eleven." His face fell. "You're not going?"

"I'll come another time."

"Whoa there! We're not mixed up in it? I've enough to cope with without the place getting a bad name."

"It won't. You're not on my list of suspects."

He marched out, with his head in the air, and Barker, starting to follow, heard, "He doesn't change. If he dislikes his job as much as that, what does he go on for?"

"You wouldn't want anyone else, would you?"

"Not me," the manager called after the detective-constable. "I'm a Gunnarshaw man too."

The Sergeant and Clive had crossed to the other side of the road, where the entrance to a bus station branched from it. Barker ran, his heart in his mouth, shouting, "Watch out!" as the red double-decked bus swerved and pulled up with a screech of brakes. Clive turned his head but the Sergeant didn't alter his pace in the slightest or diverge from the centre line of the station approach. The driver leaned out of his cab, wiping his forehead with his fingers, and said to Barker, who looked up at him, "There's one thing, he's big enough to see. But he's going to get me jailed someday. It's not that dog of his you want to put on a lead, it's him."

Cluff continued unperturbed, along the edge of the open expanse of concrete with its little roofed but wall-less shelters dotted round the perimeter, through an opening between buildings on the farther side. The right-of-way narrowed like the mouth of a funnel to outlet steps leading to a footbridge over the canal, which ran through this part of the town on its way towards the mill where Culter worked and on beyond the railway station to the open fields. Barker overtook the Sergeant on the bridge, its steel-plate sides very high, too high to see over, with strands of barbed wire strung on their tops as a precaution against small boys climbing up and falling off into the water. A solitary lamp on a bracket at the other end provided the only light there was and they could hear the diesel engines growling on the bus station but not see the buses when they looked round.

A second flight of steps, their stone treads hollowed by three generations or more of feet, brought them down to ground level, a street of stumpy cottages to their front that hadn't been built yesterday or the day before, or the day before that. The squares of lighted windows shone at intervals on the pavements: the doors were closed: a baby howled somewhere: a woman quarrelled with a man or the other way about. The great dark shapes of gasometers towered above the low roofs and the air was acrid.

They didn't continue between the cottages but instead turned left at the foot of the bridge, between it and the wall of a coal dump, on to the canal towpath. Barker thought the town was full of smells tonight, dung by the auction mart, petrol fumes in the High Street, the residue from retorts and furnaces about the cottages, here a damp foetid miasma compact of decaying matter, both animal and vegetable. Mist lay like a blanket on the water, writhing, whiter than the black dark through which they stumbled. On the far side of the canal the blank wall of a warehouse plunged straight into the depths. Some distance ahead, once they'd passed under the footbridge, eyes of twinkling light marked the whereabouts of another, wider bridge carrying a motor road. Otherwise, only the vague sheen of the water and the greyness clinging to it relieved the pitch of the night.

They lurched amongst the lumps of rock that were the foundations of the towpath, its surface long since worn away, in the days when horses still towed the barges of coal and grain, and never replaced. Liquid mud from the deep puddles they couldn't see splashed them to their knees. Rusty iron rings to which the barges had once moored, rearing from the blocks of stone in which their hinges were embedded, lay in wait to trap them. There wasn't any traffic these days on the water, no horses, only an odd cabin cruiser struggling through the weed encroaching from the banks. The stench in their nostrils came from the things it held trapped, the bloated bodies of unwanted dogs, the sacks with their mouths tightly bound that held the corpses of drowned kittens, the rotting refuse from allotments, which their owners were too lazy to burn.

The wall on their left, its base shrouded in tall grass noisome and slippery with canine faeces, merged unexpectedly with three cottages that continued its line along the towpath, relics of a past age once occupied by canal rangers. Now that they came abreast of the middle one slim pencils of light outlined the two sides and sill of a window over which a blind was drawn.

Cluff passed through a gap in a railing a foot or so from the house wall and Barker hadn't the faintest idea what they were doing here or how their visit could possibly concern the murder they were supposed to be investigating. The dull thud of the Sergeant's clenched fist on the wooden panels filled his ears and he sensed Clive's fur bristling along the ridge of the dog's spine.

He could tell it was a woman blocking the open doorway though, with the light behind her, her features remained hidden. Cluff's voice said, in a low tone, "Sally," and the figure started back, drawing together, cringing. The Sergeant walked into the house without being invited and Barker got as far as the doorway with Clive but the dog's hackles rose more and it stopped dead on the threshold, growling.

The door opened directly into a small living-room, much more neatly and comfortably furnished than Barker had expected from the situation and age of the cottage. The woman who hadn't opposed their entry, but perhaps had wanted to, stared at Cluff with an expression of horror in her eyes and a hand half raised to her parted lips, prepared to strangle the cry welling in her throat if she lost control of it. The detective-constable remembered seeing her in the High Street sometimes but he'd never taken any particular notice of her. He had a dim recollection that she used to go in and out of an entrance leading to a flight of stairs, which mounted to an upper floor occupied by a firm of solicitors and she looked like a clerk of some sort, reliable: he wouldn't have hesitated himself to trust her with the secrets of a business or confidential papers dealing with the private affairs of clients. The only sound, apart from a hiss now and again from a brightly blazing fire, was the low rumble of Clive's growling and he waited for Cluff to order the dog to silence, but without result. Little tremors ran wavelike under Clive's skin and he stood straddle-legged with his tail straight, poised. Barker stooped and slipped his fingers under the dog's collar.

If the woman had eyes for no one but the Sergeant the attention of the man in the chair on the right of the hearth was fixed on Clive. He had about him exactly the same horror-stricken attitude as she had and they were both afraid. The seconds dragged on endlessly and the woman made a little moaning sound.

"His mother?" Barker asked himself. But she was too young, not actually young, simply not old enough to have a son like that. As a matter of fact, a decision about her actual age was anything but easy. She looked tired and there were lines on her face but he thought that worry and strain could have etched them: if grey had crept amongst the strands of her dark hair her flesh seemed firm. She could have made something of her face with a proper use of cosmetics and in different clothes she would have been attractive. Her hands were innocent of rings and she wore thick-soled, sensible shoes below opaque stockings. Her dress was too long by a few inches and it didn't flatter her figure or attempt to display it. He felt drawn to her, not sexually but by something in her personality that hinted at a brave courage, well tested, a duty accepted and performed without resentment, a willingness to meet whatever trials she had uncomplainingly, putting to one side her own wishes and desires, forgetting them.

If not his mother, then certainly not his wife. A girl, in any case, would have been hard put to it for a man to take him for a husband and if she was too young for the one he was too young for the other, a difference between them, Barker reckoned, of a dozen years or so. He was long and thin and bony and his clothes hung on him loosely, his neck sprouting from a too-large collar, scrawny and with a prominent Adam's apple that jerked in a ceaseless, nervous movement. An adolescent acne covered his face and he'd scratched the spots raw and red. A down fuzzed his upper lip and soft hairs grew sparse, isolated and well spaced, under his chin and about his jaws. His large hands clutched the arms of his chair and the dog terrified him.

"Clive knows you," Cluff said, addressing the youth by the hearth. "Hasn't your sister done enough for you without having this on her shoulders too?" The woman sobbed and the Sergeant told her, "You must have tumbled to it."

"What are you going to do?" Barker heard her say, but he

had to strain his ears to catch the question.

Cluff shook his head, in the manner of a man confronted by a problem not that he found difficult of solution but whose answer he didn't want to admit.

"Arrest him?" She waited for a reply without getting any. "He can't help it. He's had no one."

"He's had you," Cluff said, through set lips.

"I couldn't be a father to him."

The youth shifted in his chair and relaxed.

"I want to talk to him," the Sergeant said, and waited. She stood her ground. "Alone."

Her eyes wandered, coming to rest finally on Barker in mute appeal. His heart twisted and he looked away, pushing the outer door to, releasing his grip on Clive, standing with his back to it.

Cluff put his hand on Sally's arm. He said softly, "Make us some tea," and led her towards a scullery. She pleaded, "Don't take him away," but he pushed her gently out of the room, closing the scullery door firmly. The hope that had crept into the youth's eyes faded.

"I wish," the Sergeant said, "they'd caught you, not to bring you to me, to take the law into their own hands, as Jack would have done last night, as his neighbours would have helped him to do. They'd have beaten you to within an inch of your life. I wouldn't have stopped them."

"I haven't done any harm."

"She's brought you up. She's worked and slaved for you ever since you were three years old. She was fifteen the year your father walked drunk into the canal. Your mother was in a sanatorium. You'd no one except your sister and even then she'd run this house from the time you were born."

"It wasn't my fault."

"And your mother never came back. There wasn't a penny. You wouldn't have had a roof over your head if the Canal Company hadn't been persuaded not to take this place away for another of its men."

The youth smirked: "Was it you, Mr Cluff?"

"And this is how you've repaid her," the Sergeant continued. "You've never held a job for more than a few weeks. The money in your pocket comes from her, the clothes on your back, the food you put into your mouth." He walked forward. "She'd be better off without you. If it hadn't been for you she might have had a husband, a family of her own—"

"Sally!" the youth exclaimed, sneering.

"Sally," the Sergeant repeated. "And I'd break her heart if I did what I ought to do." He towered over the youth, his fists clenched. "It's taking me all my time to keep my hands off you."

Barker moved noisily and Cluff glanced round at him. The Sergeant's fingers uncurled and he turned to the fire, staring at it morosely. The scullery door opened and the girl stood there but the look on Cluff's face drove her out again and the latch of the door clicked shut.

"Was it him?" Barker asked, unable to endure the silence any longer, and accused, "You recognized him. The dog recognized him." He was going to add, "And you could have caught him last night when he ran down the back street into Sevastopol Road. He wasn't too quick for you. You let him go," but he couldn't say it out loud.

"She's never thought about it," the Sergeant said. "There

wasn't anyone else and she had to do it. She doesn't even know what she's given up, what she could have had, what she ought to have had."

"Why do you pick on me?" the youth whined. "If you knew some of the things I'd seen——"

"Up there on the hill?" Cluff said, and "You can't," Barker objected silently. "We don't want to know. What they do in the privacy of their houses isn't our business. If it was, this isn't the way to find out about it."

"The people with money, the people who pass you in the street with their noses in the air, your friends, Mr Cluff."

"Who said they were friends of mine?"

"With their wives, with women who aren't their wives."

"They're all married behind the windows through which you peeped."

"Is Culter? What do you want me for? I've not done anything. He's got a woman in the house."

"Hasn't anyone told you, there's such a thing as love——?"

"Like that? I saw him, coming into the room behind her, kissing her——" His voice trailed regretfully away.

"But I couldn't stay, there was someone coming. I didn't need to stay, I knew what would happen next."

"Your father had the same sort of mind."

"It's always me," the youth complained. "Or people like me. The ones with money can get away with anything. You're safe with me, aren't you? I can't fight back."

"It's beyond my reckoning," Cluff said, "how a girl like Sally comes to be your sister." He went to the scullery door and opened it: "We're going."

"Your tea?" and the girl looked at her brother in the chair

as if she couldn't believe he was still there.

"Not this time," the Sergeant murmured. "But it's the only chance he'll get," and he looked her straight in the eyes.

"I'll see he behaves himself," she promised. "I'll never be able to thank you."

"It's not me you have to thank, it's yourself."

"I don't deserve it: I should have done more for him."

"It's up to him now. No one knows except us."

"I'll try harder."

"He's the one who has to try."

The Sergeant stalked past Barker, out of the front door on to the canal bank, and Clive went after him. Barker looked at the girl and said finally, "You can rely on me: I won't say anything." He pulled the door to on an absolute silence and joined Cluff in the night.

They set off in the direction of the road bridge, under whose arch the path narrowed dangerously and plunged almost to the level of the water. They came through it to a sort of quay, with a wide space running up to the road, its approach open, not blocked off by a wall or fence. A small crane faced a Company warehouse across the canal and a repair and storage depot, alongside which a maintenance barge was moored astern of a half-sunk icebreaker.

The Sergeant stopped. He asked, as much of the night as of Barker: "What would it have done to her if I'd taken him in?" and added, after a long pause. "Everything she's sacrificed – to have that for her only compensation, the publicity, the scandal plastered in the newspapers, a brother in prison, and when he comes out! They'd sooner forgive murder in Gunnarshaw. They'd never stop remembering what he'd done, or talking about it."

The towpath started again round the corner of a building carrying the sign of a wholesale fruiterer. "Go home," Cluff said. "We've done enough for tonight," and Barker watched him and Clive disappear along the canal bank.

The detective-constable stood for some time, thinking, a little troubled, before he went up to the road and to his lodgings.

CHAPTER VIII

The Duty Constable ruled off yesterday's entries in the Complaints Book and filled in the new date. A bright, sterile sunlight shone coldly through a window from whose lower edge a film of hoar frost climbed whitely, halfway up to the top of the lower sash. He reached under his tunic and pulled the home-knitted pullover he wore farther down to his belly, which outdid the Sergeant's in size. Little drops of moisture glistened amongst the bristles of his moustache: a florid man, the tip of his nose was purple in colour this morning. He yawned and stretched and looked at the clock on the wall. After a while he came through the flap in the counter and walked into the corridor between the doors of Inspector Mole's office and the C.I.D. room.

Barker came in from the street, a scarf round his neck, breathing quickly, like a man who'd been hurrying. He glanced at the empty office and went to the C.I.D. room, whose door he opened. It was empty too and he couldn't see amongst the litter on Cluff's table any sign of morning mail, but that wasn't unusual. From behind him the Duty Constable said, "I didn't think you'd be in."

"The Sergeant?"

"Hasn't turned up. It's slipped your mind? He's got a murderer to catch."

The constable carried a thick china mug, from out of which a little cloud of steam drifted. He walked back behind the counter, holding the mug in both hands, his palms pressed against it, almost hiding it: "Haven't you got a topcoat?"

"It's fine."

"For once. They probably have a fine day or two at the North Pole: it doesn't mean they go about in bathing costumes." He sucked at his tea. "The kettle's just boiled if you want me to brew some for you."

"I'm warm enough."

"You have to say so." The tea scalded his tongue. "Where did you get to last night?"

"Yes, where?" and Inspector Mole had arrived in the office, quietly, walking on his rubber soles, in his greatcoat, his hands gloved, shoes highly polished, looking very neat and businesslike. The Duty Constable grinned widely and the Inspector was suspicious of a joke but unable to put his finger on it.

"Nowhere," Barker said.

"What? Hasn't he roped anybody in yet? I made sure he'd have it all buttoned up by now." He noted the constable's mug. "Dinner already?" he asked, "Or a second breakfast? It's as well we have to have a man on the counter. With a figure like yours you wouldn't be much good on patrol." He turned to Barker. "A bit different – eh? – when it isn't a local. The Sergeant's at a disadvantage this time, no personal knowledge to give him a head start. We'll see what happens when it's the same for all of us."

"Tell us about it, Inspector," the Duty Constable said, innocently.

"A lot of good that'd be. Women aren't in it with you when it comes to gossip," and Mole walked off into his room.

The Duty Constable waited for his door to close before he pulled a copy of a morning paper from under the counter. "They've got a list of his neighbours in here. Nothing pleases them better than to see their names in print but not in this sort of connexion. Which of them do you reckon it was?"

"Ask the Sergeant."

No one came into the station: no one went out of it: the Inspector's door stayed firmly shut. The clock ticked loudly and the film of hoar frost on the window diminished little by little. Barker leaned against the counter on one side, his finger drumming on its top, and the Duty Constable leaned against it on the other.

"You could give him a ring at the cottage," the constable suggested, but Barker made no move for the telephone.

The clock ticked on. The constable turned the pages of his Complaints Book, bored, and glanced at the entries: "It's an ill wind," he remarked. "This chap who's been looking in at windows'll have a field day. There's a bit more to bother about now than a Peeping Tom." He let his mind work and the process could be read on his face. "It couldn't have been him? Or was there a pair of them? I've been tempted myself to find out just what does go on in those houses on the hill." He nodded at Mole's door. "The Inspector's included. They can't keep it up all the time, surely, the way they walk about the town as if butter wouldn't melt in their mouths." His thoughts ran away with him. "Blackmail perhaps? Caleb wouldn't be put off if it was one of them. There's no love lost there."

"Mole wouldn't like it."

"It wouldn't harm him," and the constable's hand wandered from his scalp to his nostrils. "Not that all of his neighbours are out of the top drawer—" and his voice stopped abruptly. He didn't say anything for a moment or two, and then, "Is that what's worrying Caleb?"

"Stick to your counter."

"Bright Culter's not my cup of tea," the constable said, "but, when all's said and done, he's one of us."

"What's that about Culter?" and the Inspector was standing in his doorway. He watched Barker turn away from the counter and walk for the street, and it took time before he asked the constable, "He's been talking to you?"

"He's nothing to talk about."

"I wonder," the Inspector said, a shrewd expression in his eyes. "Is that the way the wind's blowing?" His door closed but it reopened almost at once and he had his cap on his head again, his coat on his back. He fastened his buttons and started to pull on his gloves as he crossed the office.

The proprietor of the fruit stall on the setts in the High Street said, "He's not here. I haven't seen hide nor hair of him this morning, nor yesterday either for that matter."

The mouth of the ginnel that was the Sergeant's usual post, across the pavement from the stalls, yawned, deserted, and women glanced askance at it as they passed with their shopping bags. Faces peered from the windows of the offices above the shops on the opposite side of the street, one of them, Barker imagined, belonging to the girl on whom he'd called with Cluff last night.

"It takes a killing to pry him loose from that ginnel," the

man at the stall said. "He won't turn up again, not till this is over. He never does."

"You know all about it," Barker replied.

"Get your skates on," the hawker advised. "Caleb'll have it all worked out before you catch up with him."

He didn't look back as he turned the corner by the church, so he failed to see Mole's red minicar driving slowly up the street. In front of him the hill climbed through the outskirts of the older part of the town and crossed a green belt to those new houses of its most select suburb on the top. The way to Cluff's cottage tempted him but he couldn't be sure that the Sergeant would welcome his company. This wasn't like the incident in the backyard behind Balaclava Street. You couldn't stretch the law in a matter of murder and he'd no shadow of doubt in his mind that the Sergeant would ever consider it, but duty wasn't always pleasant or performed without a struggle and men could be driven by desperation to deeds they'd never have imagined except in moments of insanity. Who was the victim, the dead or the living, the killed or the killer? What the youth had said in the cottage by the canal worried him and he'd been wrong to think, even for a moment, they'd put the major crime on one side in favour of the minor one.

He swung left along a main road, in the direction of the Secondary Modern School of which Rigsby had charge. After half a mile or so the park lay over the ridge to his left and the street on his right, like the road he'd forsworn for this one, led, too, to those detached and semi-detached houses occupied by Gunnarshaw's *élite*. He stopped at its corner and looked at his watch, surprised to find that the morning was so little advanced. Nailed boots beat a tattoo on the pavement and a day like this, after so many of rain and wind, should have made him feel cheerful. The crisp, clear air tasted like wine in his throat: the sun, even if it had no warmth, was brilliant in a blue sky pocked only by a few snow-white clouds, like washed fleeces. The branches of the trees in the grounds of a former workhouse shed their last remaining leaves, which floated gently, displaying a galaxy of colour, russet and gold, and drifted soundlessly to the ground.

"It's grand," the postman said, coming up to him, "but we deserve it."

"It should have come earlier in the year."

"We can't have it as we like: there'd be a bonny old mix-up if we could." His empty bag jostled his hip, pushed towards the small of his back, and he looked a picture of health, the red on his uniform sparkling like his face, his cap on one side of his head. He had a stub of cigarette between his lips and the appearance of a man with a job well done.

"Finished?" Barker said.

"I started off at seven."

"It's a bit lighter now than it would be then," Barker said, glancing at the bag.

"This round's no cop," the postman complained. "By the letters they get they must spend half their lives writing." He took a last drag at the cigarette and flung it away. "Any nearer?"

Barker looked up at the sky.

"A pity he wasn't in the front garden," the postman remarked. "I'd have found him yesterday half-an-hour before anybody else did. They aren't early risers in this district. I doubt if they've ever seen the sun coming up, most of them."

He kicked idly at the uneven flagstones. "If you leave out Bright Culter, of course, but he has to be off early to the mill."

"He won't add much to the weight you've got to carry."

"Who'd write to him? He's never hardly set foot out of this town and no one here'd waste stamps on a letter, even if he had friends."

"He's got somebody to talk to now, at any rate."

"I could do with more like him. He takes her letters for her when he meets me in the road."

"Saves you walking to his door."

"It's all right with me if she's prepared to wait for her mail until he gets back at dinner-time. Not that there's much."

"I don't know her."

"You've missed nowt – or maybe you have," and a smile played over the postman's lips. "There's something to be said for having a woman like that on tap."

"Not Culter."

"He doesn't know what to do with his money, and she knows her way about."

"She didn't learn it in Gunnarshaw."

"Not her! I can just see her in Lime Street – with a sailor on her arm, coming out of a pub."

"Lime Street?"

"I'm not blind. Her letters are postmarked Liverpool."

"So that's why the Sergeant went to the ticket office," Barker thought, and said, "You've been talking to Caleb Cluff."

"Me? I haven't set eyes on him for a week," and the postman went off down the main road, in the direction of a little red car parked by the kerb. Inspector Mole put his head out of its window and called him over.

Now and again as they talked the postman glanced back and then the car started. It swung into the side road at the corner of which Barker was standing and drove by without stopping though Mole put his hand up in greeting, a smug expression on his face. It occurred to the detective-constable with increasing force that innocence combined with money didn't mix with experience and he was angry with himself, certain that the Inspector had followed him, that the postman had repeated his gossip. He felt that he'd let the Sergeant down and he wanted Cluff to do things in his own way, softening the blow, if it had to fall, with no complications from Mole. Any lingering intention he'd had of going to the Sergeant's cottage evaporated and had he made matters worse instead of better?

CHAPTER IX

Mrs Mole, a cloth tied round her head like a turban, wearing her cleaning clothes and stockings with ladders in them, lay full length under the bed, dusting the surround between the wall and the carpet at its head. She recognized the sound of the engine and squirmed backwards, arching her rump, pulling off her head-tie and taking a quick glance in the dressing-table mirror before she went to the window. The car wasn't drawn up by their gate but at Culter's and the Inspector had his finger on the bellpush of the house next door. The housekeeper opened it and he disappeared inside.

They faced each other in the hall and he tried not to admit that she had her points, young but not too young, mature yet not over-ripe, comparing favourably with his wife. "About the murder?" she asked, and he agreed wordlessly. She said, "A man in plain clothes came yesterday."

He pulled his copy of the victim's photograph from his pocket: "Do you know him?"

"Why should I?"

She disappointed him a little, her glance too casual, the implication of her ignorance too offhand: "It's a routine question." He watched her clasped hands, the fingers twisting. "Your friends," he said, "how often do they write to you?" and he believed her astonishment genuine. "You must receive letters sometimes."

"I don't understand."

"A widow?" he murmured.

"My husband was lost at sea."

"A bad business."

"It was a long time ago."

She showed him to the door and as he turned into his own drive he caught sight of his wife at the window of their bedroom. He rang up the police station and in answer to his question the Duty Constable replied, "No, he still hasn't come in," and then, "Hold on – Barker's just got back." The Inspector put the receiver down on its rest without waiting and from the stairs Mrs Mole said, coldly, "I wouldn't put it past her."

"Don't be silly."

"What's silly about it?" and he'd annoyed her. "Culter's worth marrying."

"She'd have to keep her eyes shut."

"You're a fool. It's his money she's after," and her gaze was as cold as her voice.

"Why don't you leave it to me?"

"A man!" and her tone withered him.

He said quickly, "He could have got a daily woman in. If he had to have a housekeeper he could have picked somebody older."

"And had to kill to keep her?"

"You don't know everything."

"It amazes me. How did you manage to get promotion?"

"He's never been married."

"At an awkward age, I suppose?"

"Isn't he?"

"About yours."

"You don't know what you're talking about," and Mole started for the door. "I've work to do."

She hadn't moved from the stairs. "Naturally," she said. "Sergeant Cluff would be lost without you to put him right."

He tried to restrain himself but he couldn't: "Sergeant Cluff," he hissed, "doesn't seem to care one way or the other – probably because it happened just over my hedge," and he spoilt the effect by banging the door so hard he drowned the sound of his own voice.

The gears of his car scraped and he drove fast, seething inwardly, until the spatter of mud on the paintwork and a violent jolting reminded him of his springs. He slowed to a crawl up the lane, more angry than ever.

The Sergeant's derelict, bull-nosed, two-seater Morris leered at him from its shed as he trod mincingly up the garden path, between the patches of lawn and the flowerbeds. Hens clucked busily, enjoying the sun, under the nude trees of the orchard, and sheep cropped the sparse grass in a pasture beyond it. The moors looked very high and very close, their details sharp and clean-cut in the clear light. A plume of smoke curled from the chimney and the diamond-shaped panes in the mullioned windows winked at him.

Annie Croft, her welcome cool, took him into the living-room, where Cluff, in his carpet slippers, sat smoking, Jenet on his knee, Clive stretched on the rug at his feet.

"We couldn't find you in Gunnarshaw," Mole said, a little shocked at the pallor of the Sergeant's face, at its weariness, the pouches under the eyes, its deeply etched furrows.

"You sent off that photograph and his fingerprints. Haven't you and Patterson got it all in hand?"

The Inspector kept his temper: "Culter's housekeeper comes from Liverpool."

"You live next door to her: you must have heard her speaking."

"She got letters from there."

Cluff straightened suddenly: the cat jumped from his lap and Clive sat up on his haunches.

"At least," Mole said, enjoying his triumph, "they were addressed to her. Whether they ever came into her possession's another kettle of fish."

Annie Croft thrust her head round the door, the bunch of artificial fruit on the brim of her hat quivering: "I'm off home. Your dinner's in the oven."

"Something's upset her?" the Inspector asked.

"You."

"I know I don't come here often," and Mole sounded offended.

Cluff stared at him and offered an olive branch: "I've tried her this morning. She doesn't approve of me moping."

The Inspector let it go: "Culter collected them. I've seen him myself with the postman in the road." He paused for effect. "I've talked to her. He didn't hand them over."

"Some women are liars."

"Putting it off won't get you anywhere."

"Only one person amongst your neighbours it could be," Cluff said, bitter again. "Your friends don't go in for murder."

"Look at it: it stands to reason. Over the hedge from his garden. Think about the life he's led."

"Neither do mine," the Sergeant said.

"The letters!"

"You've only her word. Bright's as honest as the day." He lapsed into thought. "You didn't know his mother well: I did. I've no illusions about the way he was raised." He leaned forward and tapped the bowl of his pipe on the bars of the grate with a gesture of finality.

The blood surged to the Inspector's cheeks: "See here——"

"She's made an impression on you."

"That's ridiculous. His head was bashed in. He was stabbed for good measure."

"You saw the body. He wasn't as big as Hilda Smith. He wasn't as heavy."

"She's a woman."

The Sergeant got to his feet: "What sort of a connexion had Bright with a man like that? What reason had he to kill him?"

"Something to do with those letters——"

"A guess."

"You've thought of another motive?" and the question was rhetorical.

"Is it so difficult?"

"He wanted more than a housekeeper."

"And wouldn't offer less than marriage or believe that she'd accept less."

"Then why the devil are we arguing?"

"Must I spell it out?" and the tiredness in Cluff's voice was an insult.

"Make an idiot of yourself in your own way," Inspector Mole replied, his temper fraying at last, and suddenly remembered those other cases of Cluff's in which they'd been at odds. He strode for the passage, trying to hold on to his confidence, consoling himself that he'd done his best, convinced that this time he was right. But if he proved wrong again?

Jenet leapt back into Cluff's vacant chair: Clive stood up, his tail wagging. The Sergeant moved a little from the hearth, vaguely conscious of a need for apology, and what did it matter? The engine of the car in the lane started, hummed for a while, getting farther and farther away, and then faded altogether.

He turned back to the fire and put an arm on the mantel, leaning there, recognizing the signs in himself, to tolerate them harder not easier with each new involvement. He wanted with all his heart to escape from this, these pursuits and captures, the inevitability of the courts that followed, the sentences that imprisoned some part of himself with those who stood in the dock. They wouldn't go free, whether he or another sat in the C.I.D. room at the police station, and it wasn't right that they should. He could be sorry for them but the law was still the law. Weakness wasn't any excuse, or suffering, or desperation, though the causes twisted the heartstrings. It didn't end with them or with the effect on him. No one lived in a vacuum and the people they left behind them had to go on existing. Sometimes, if the hurt had been negligible, if the crime wouldn't be repeated, he could do it, as he had done for Sally in that house on the canal bank, but murder was irrevocable and he couldn't do it for Bright.

He lifted his eyes from the fire. Clive rubbed gently against his legs. His eyes wandered round the comfortable room, with its chintz at the window and bright on the upholstered furniture, with its black-oak table and sideboard and its corner cupboards behind whose glass-panelled doors porcelain shone delicately white and tinted on the shelves, with its brasses on the walls that reflected both sunlight and fire-glow, its rough-hewn, square beams carrying the planks that floored the bedroom above. He wasted these hours he spent here, the decision unavoidable, an alternative non-existent.

He didn't know how long Annie had been watching him, her hands on her hips, her feet firmly planted, her hat and coat discarded. He said, "I thought you'd gone."

"Did you want the Inspector to stay?"

"Where were you?"

"The kitchen."

"He didn't speak softly."

"Neither did you."

"You heard then."

"It wasn't Bright Culter?"

"No."

"Someone else from Gunnarshaw?"

He shook his head.

"What are you worried about?" She waited. "That woman?"

"Maybe."

"Mole doesn't think so."

"What the Inspector thinks isn't possible." He turned away. "But Bright could be in love with her."

"He's not capable of knowing what love is, not after a life like his."

"What will it do to him when I take her away?"

"He'll thank you for it later."

"You don't believe that. To him she might be everything

he's ever longed for, everything he's dreamed about—"

"You're doing him a favour."

"He'll never agree."

"There's no doubt about it?"

"I don't see how there can be."

"Those letters Mole mentioned?"

"I wish he'd never told me."

She said, "Then you've got to do it."

"Pack me a bag."

"What!"

"Contact Barker," he told her, "when I've gone. He'll look after Clive: you see to the cat."

CHAPTER X

Dusk drew in early at this time of the year. The light through
the window of the outer office at the police station had a
quality of steel about it, as hard and indestructible, as metallic.
The sky remained clear, clearer than it had been all day, the
few clouds dancing attendance on the sun sinking with it
below the horizon. The temperature dropped and the evening
gave promise of another frost: a single star already shone.

The Duty Constable flung his pencil on the counter and
swore: "I'd rather it was raining."

Barker felt it too, the contrast between the sterile, clean
butt-end of the afternoon and the sordidness of violent death,
between the purity of the natural world and the beastliness of
men and women, with their animal urges, their impulses to
mating, the whole rottenness in which they wallowed, pigs
in their own filth. He leaned on the counter because he'd
nowhere else to go, not because he enjoyed the company of
the constable: there were too many people in the world he
couldn't avoid, too many thoughts he couldn't rebuff.

"He's been sulking ever since this morning," the constable
grumbled. "We're all in for it. It's about as much as flesh and
blood can stand."

Not a sound came from behind the door of the Inspector's
room and it might have been unoccupied but they knew it

wasn't. "I don't envy his wife," the constable added, "nor his children. It's a wonder to me how they put up with him." Now that he'd started to speak he found it difficult to stop. "Why can't he keep his finger out of it? Is he frightened someone's going to get ahead of him? It's Caleb's case. He's had everything solved before – to his own satisfaction not to anybody else's. Won't he ever learn? He can't see the wood for the trees. Heaven help the innocent when he pokes his nose in."

"But he could be right this time," Barker thought, and didn't Cluff think so as well or why would he have shut himself up, refusing to face them, trying to bring himself to the point of action against a man he'd grown up with, whose life he knew almost as well as his own? Wasn't there any other reason for killing except the pursuit of women by men and the promiscuity of the female, the lasciviousness of the male, the jealousies and the passions, the hates and the cruelties inherent in the sexual relationship? Not in Gunnarshaw, he told himself, and his heart sank at the picture of the town the Sergeant tried to maintain, against all reason, when the reality was so different. People here were the same as anywhere else, worse perhaps, because they'd less opportunity to gratify their lusts, driven to a competition that could only end in disaster, compelled to their own destruction by the hypocritical veneer of a small-town society.

"What makes them do it?" the constable asked, echoing Barker's thoughts. "They're worse in their forties and fifties than they are in their twenties. It's always women, women, women – women from birth to a man's dying day. We shouldn't have to bear it. Someone's made a poor job of creating mankind, loading it with this sort of thing."

Had man a choice? Who or what drove him to these acts? But what was choice without the strength of will to repel temptation except illusion? Cluff wasn't wrong, the Inspector wasn't wrong, none of them were wrong. Always, as the constable said, a woman, a nude, unfeathered, unfurred, forked creature whose only beauty existed in her function of procreation, colourless, crude, physically botched and unbalanced. Look at her dispassionately and what was there to see, what adornments did she have except those she created for herself to conceal the truth about her nakedness? And men killed for this, men fought, men threw overboard their dignity, men competed for a prize not only worthless in itself but duplicated a million times, every woman like the next, the only distinction in her availability or the possibility of her surrender.

That youth in the cottage by the canal, telling them about Culter: Culter in the night after the cinema closed: Culter a man who'd lived without a woman: Culter driven to protect his dream against a rival – the thoughts crowded into Barker's brain, and what was the constable staring at? He looked over his shoulder and gaped too, at Annie Croft and a despondent Clive. "He told me to let you have the dog," she said. "I had to come into Gunnarshaw to the shops."

"What's happened to him?"

"He's gone away," and she walked out, leaving Clive with his tail drooping and his head hanging.

The light faded more, the shadows thickening, the office darker. They heard a car draw up outside and watched the door. This had gone too far to stop: they'd lost control of events and nothing remained except the conclusion.

The big man who came in wore an overcoat over a city suit. He had a clipped, military moustache and a commanding bearing, clear eyes, and a calmness about him, both of manner and expression. Barker shuffled uneasily and the constable moved slowly for the light switches. The door of Mole's office opened to admit the Inspector and the dog couldn't make up its mind which of them to go to for sympathy.

"Caleb?" Chief Superintendent Patterson said. He waited and nodded, then walked to the door of the C.I.D. room, opening it and clicking on the lights inside. Barker came to life and followed and Clive passed him. When he entered the dog was lying under Cluff's table, its head on its extended forepaws, and Patterson sat in the Sergeant's chair, hat on the tattered blotting pad.

"He's not ill?" the Chief Superintendent asked, and Barker shook his head miserably. "But the dog's with you," Patterson said.

The door closed and Inspector Mole was in the room too. The Superintendent stared at him past Barker: "It was you who sent those fingerprints and photographs?"

"We have to know who the dead man is."

"I couldn't see Caleb's touch in it." He regarded Barker with a quizzical expression: "It was a fine afternoon and I'd finished early. I'm not here to spy on you."

"They want action," the Inspector murmured.

"The citizens of Gunnarshaw?"

"It's two days now."

"Well?"

The Inspector opened his mouth to release the words welling in his throat and he shut it again, a difference between the certainty he felt and bringing it out into the open. He couldn't trust

the Sergeant and why should he make a fool of himself? Was
the parade of his brilliance and efficiency worth the damage
to his reputation in the remote possibility that somewhere,
inconceivably, all wasn't as he believed? It was one thing to talk
to Cluff at the cottage, another to insist to the Superintendent
that he knew the criminal. His wife brought up too often the
mistakes of the past and this man in the Sergeant's chair, with
a look about him of the Sergeant that defied the difference
in their dress, also came, in his origins, from Gunnarshaw,
however long it was since he'd left it. He'd a suspicion that
Patterson could read him like a book and he heard, "I like to
come back now and again. There's nothing to see from my
window at Headquarters except chimneys and smoke."

Barker reached into the file dip and picked up the single
cover it contained. The Superintendent moved his hat to one
side and put the file on the blotter. He opened it and read its
one enclosure, a half sheet of typing, its text the only clue that
the scrawled signature was Doctor Hamm's.

"A knife isn't a woman's weapon," Mole stated, breaking
the silence.

"Is it a woman then?"

"The Sergeant's got it into his head."

"He's said so?"

"She's not Gunnarshaw."

"A pity – for her."

"From Liverpool," Barker said. "Or she has friends there.
So was the dead man." The Inspector stiffened. "He had the
accent," Barker continued. "Someone took a ticket from there
the day before we found him."

"Does it affect your case, Inspector?" Patterson asked.

"I'm always the last to know. It isn't in the file. What are records for?"

"The Sergeant would have told you, perhaps."

"She's not old. She lives with a man called Bright Culter."

"Culter?" and the Superintendent considered. "I only remember one family of that name. His wife?"

"Perhaps she hopes to be. She calls herself his housekeeper."

"Attractive?"

"He might think so."

"Enough to kill for her?"

"It's Cluff's business. I give what help I can," the Inspector said.

The Superintendent sat for a while before reaching for the telephone and dialling the exchange, asking for his party by name not by number. He identified himself when his call came through and said what he wanted. He listened and then: "It's not important but if he contacts you again tell him I've been ringing." He replaced the receiver. "They couldn't help the Sergeant. Your victim isn't known to the police in his home town." He got to his feet and looked at his watch: "I ought to be getting back: not that forty miles is far and my wife's away." He turned to Barker. "You live in lodgings still? I need a meal first. Come and join me." He smiled. "We'll take the dog. It'll set the town speculating." He grinned at Mole. "You'll keep an eye on the house next door to you?" and explained, "I'm not psychic. Your driver told me when he brought the photographs the geography of the crime and more than one of your local celebrities has been in touch. Your neighbours didn't expect anything like this with a policeman living amongst them. In any case, it's all in the papers."

CHAPTER XI

He still had in his pocket the photograph he'd picked up from where Barker had put it on the counter in Fred's café. His feet hurt him, the pavements hard and unyielding, not like those in Gunnarshaw, no relief from them to the softness of the grass verges as he went home to his cottage. The smoke and the smell of the buses he travelled in, directed from one police station to the next, wearied him and the use of Patterson's name hadn't helped. They'd told him everlastingly they'd no information to give him, that they'd confirmed this already in answer to the Chief Superintendent's circulated query, but he wouldn't be satisfied, insisting on his own check, showing the photograph, working outwards from the centre of the city, taking the poorer suburbs first.

Gulls wheeled and screeched above his head: the sirens of ships hooted now and again from the river. When he looked over the roofs a tracery of masts and funnels loomed against the background of the sky. The cold sea wind bit through the worn material of his Burberry and snatched at his tweed hat. The walking-stick he carried was an oddity here and youths gathered in pointless groups on street-corners sneered at him. Patrolling constables, with no knowledge of his identity, frowned when they caught sight of him and watched him out of view, undecided whether or not to stop him and demand an explanation of his business. In the stations it took time to convince the desk sergeants he was one of them, with an equivalent rank. They hardly glanced at his photograph and he began to doubt whether they really believed in his murder. When he noticed his reflection in the window of some shop he was passing he couldn't blame them but neither did he envy them. He watched the people on the pavements, the sailors and the tarts, the teddy-boys, studying their faces and their dress, and he was glad he didn't have to work here. Gunnarshaw tugged at him and he hadn't decided whether he wanted to fail or succeed but he kept on stubbornly. Which was preferable, to prove her guilty and take her away from Culter or not to be able to prove it, leaving her with Bright although she was a murderess?

He'd lost count of his calls, this the fourth or maybe the fifth, and he was in the heart of the docks now, well away from the centre of the city, amongst the slums that hadn't yet been cleared and the open areas where bombs had fallen all those years ago. They stared at the photograph together and the uniformed sergeant behind the desk shook his head as all the others had done: "There's dozens like him. I wish there weren't. It's something that there's one less." A constable came along a corridor, ready to resume his beat, and the desk sergeant called him over but he wasn't much assistance either at first. He thought for a while and said, "I could have seen him. It's hard to tell." He saw the look on Cluff's face. "There's something familiar about him," and he wrinkled his brow. "It isn't me he wants," he told his sergeant, "nor you, but there's one man who'd know, if anybody does."

"It's worth trying," the desk sergeant said, after they'd

listened to him. "You can't lose by it, anyway." He glanced at the constable. "It's on his beat. He'll take you."

They talked of this and that as they walked, of the country and pensions and retirement, arriving in time at a house in a terrace, one of the best in the bad lot comprising this district. "He went on with us as long as he could," the constable said, as he knocked at a door, "and then they had to lever him out." He explained to the man who answered him what Cluff was doing there and then left them together.

The Sergeant had a fellow-feeling with this retired policeman, running to fat and grey, who led him down a passage in which a white raincoat and a peaked uniform cap hung from hooks in the wall. "I fill in time," his host said, "by being a school traffic warden. It keeps me in touch with the people," and took him into a living-room at the back of the house, sitting him in an armchair by the fire. "My wife died a few years back. I live by myself," and he set about brewing tea.

"They couldn't do anything for me at the station," Cluff said.

"I walked these streets for over thirty years. I put more than one grandfather of the children I see across the roads away. If they haven't got worse, they haven't improved much."

Cluff pulled out his photograph, a little cracked by now: "We found him with his head stove in." He wanted to put a name to the man. "What do I call you?"

"Ringer. Everybody does," and the ex-constable looked at the photograph on his way to the kettle with the teapot. "You came to the right shop."

Cluff's heart jumped: "It took me long enough."

"He was getting on for thirty," Ringer said, "and they

christened him Alphonsus Todd. He'd five sisters and seven brothers because his mother was a Catholic and so was his father, but if they hadn't been they'd not have known about birth control. Those were the ones that lived, in three rooms in a house they demolished just in time to stop it falling down on its own. His father was a docker when he worked. The children might have been his or not: he didn't worry too much. The mother wasn't particular and going to bed was the only amusement she had." He handed the Sergeant a cup of tea. "He learnt about the police early. He was in trouble before he was ten but you don't keep fingerprints of children and in those days, anyway, kids got away with a lot. The war was on and it covered a multitude of sins."

"It's since I'm interested in."

"You look like a night's rest."

"I wouldn't sleep."

"I can show you."

They finished their tea first and when they went out into the street Ringer closed his front door but he didn't trouble to lock it. They marched shoulder to shoulder along the pavement, blocking it effectively with their combined bulk, out of the narrower, darker streets into a wider, better-lit artery that it would have been kinder to leave in shadow. The strident notes of untuned pianos merged with a confusion of voices behind the windows of garish pubs. Ancient harridans, their grey locks streaming, foul-mouthed and ridiculed, lurched drunken from doors opening to crowded bars fogged in tobacco smoke, perfumed with beer and stout. Coloured men, black and yellow, brown, intoxicated in a different way with the independence of their countries, disputed with their white counterparts the favours of painted women between sixteen and sixty, who quarrelled for custom amongst themselves. It seemed to the Sergeant, until he remembered that this was exactly the setting in which he'd imagined Hilda Smith, that he'd been here before.

"Your friend Alphonsus, lived on women like those," Ringer said. "He started with one of his sisters. They weren't fastidious in his family but animals have as few secrets from each other."

"He'd that look about him."

"They didn't stay with him long. He wasn't strong enough to keep them."

"I'd like to meet someone he knew."

"It'll cost you money."

The artificial smile faded from the face of the girl Ringer fastened on and his big hand on her arm held her prisoner. They stood together while she talked, islanded, the crowds flowing round them, and then she was walking away, tripping with a clack of stiletto heels, the tightness of her skirt about her hips compelling her to tiny steps, her unwashed legs bare and veined, crumpled toes with lacquered nails protruding through the sandal fronts of her shoes.

"She could be right," Ringer said. "At least it's as good a place as any," and they went on, out of the main street into a backwater, where they found a little pub that hardly merited the name. Its tables were mostly unoccupied, the reason for its decline evident in the lack of custom, its lack of custom the cause of its comfortless appointments and the absence of chromium and glass, a vicious circle the man behind the bar couldn't break. A woman who'd long ago forgotten what it was to be young pawed a messboy who could have been her son if age had had anything to do with it and Ringer stood over them, pointing at Cluff: "He wants to talk to you."

"I'm busy," she replied.

"Get rid of him," but the boy, pale-faced and looking sick, had already seized the chance to escape. He scuttled for the door, meeting nobody's eyes, as though he couldn't quite believe his luck and wanted to get out before he pushed it too far.

"I have to eat," the woman said, in a flat voice. "Do you want me to starve?" and "She's the one?" Cluff asked Ringer.

"She was."

"You've done enough for me. I'll find my own way back."

"Whoever killed Todd," Ringer said, "don't be too hard on him," and the woman started.

The Sergeant waited till the door closed before he spoke and the man behind the bar watched them sadly, sympathetic but not to the point of a warning. "Where can we go?" Cluff asked.

"Not with you."

"How much is it worth?" The well-filled wallet made her eyes gleam. "More," he added, "than you'd earn in a week – if you earn anything at all. Boys like that can't be easy to find."

"What did Ringer mean?"

"He knows I've stayed behind with you. The barman's had a good look at me too."

She was even older on her feet than when seated, her legs shaky, her shoulders bent, grey hair straying from under a toque, body lathlike from too few meals eaten too irregularly, nervously exhausted from abuse and lack of sleep. She simpered mechanically and her sagging flesh, the ugliness in her eyes, the worn out envelope in which she kept the divine spark of humanity, filled him with nausea. He wanted to turn tail and run and after this the moors and the dales wouldn't seem so sweet.

They passed a dozen spots where they could have talked in privacy but he went on with her. On the stairs he'd a feeling that life had been too good for him, that he ought to see in reality what he'd only read about or imagined. Did he lack experience after all the years he'd been in Gunnarshaw? Had Patterson humoured him too much by posting him there originally and agreeing with his objections to a transfer? What sort of policeman was he to know so little?

The photograph wasn't necessary any more but he showed it to her all the same and it wasn't pretty, because death never is. The wound showed only slightly on the full face view and he couldn't forget the rockery stones so conveniently to hand in Culter's garden just over the fence. Where in Gunnarshaw could he have walked into an ironmonger's and come out with so sharp and slender a blade as Hamm had described? But in a port, to which seamen sailed from all parts of the world—? If this murder hadn't been fully premeditated, what of the meeting prior to it? Hadn't the killer, at least, gone prepared for any eventuality?

The expression on her face told its own story, but was she sorry or glad? Death didn't move her or make her afraid and he'd an idea she might welcome it for herself. The attic to which they'd climbed stank, of her, of the few clients too drunk to notice she'd inveigled there, of dirt and sweat and staleness. The handle of a chamber-pot protruded from under the unmade double bed, its springs crushed, its posts angled inwards, copper knobs, verdigrised, ornamenting its iron frame. A cracked wash-hand basin fitted the cutout circle of a wooden toilet stand. Matches and the disintegrating stub of a cigarette, leaking strands of tobacco like worms, discoloured the water in an ewer on the floor. Such clothes as she had apart from those she stood up in dangled from nails driven into the walls, in plain sight, and she didn't possess, apparently, either a wardrobe or a chest of drawers. A bare table and a single upright chair totalled, with the bed and the washstand, the sum of her furniture. The roof sloped either way from its ridge and rain coming in through the slates had mottled with brown patches, darker in their middles, shading through lighter browns towards their circumferences, the sheets of ceiling board insecurely attached to the rotting joists.

"He got what he deserved," she said, without emotion. "I kept him for years. He didn't care. He made me go out all night and every night, in any weather. In between, when he wanted me he took me."

"And threw you over?"

"We don't last for ever."

"How did he find out where she was?" A shadow passed over her face and for the first time her dull eyes flickered. "Was it through you?"

No drawers, no cupboards, nothing in which she could hide her possessions, only her scuffed, patent-leather handbag, its polish dimmed, and a battered fibre suitcase on the boards at the other side of the bed. He stretched out his hand, taking the bag from her without resistance, and she watched him apathetically as he tipped its contents on to the table. She was an old woman sitting there in the harsh glare of an unshaded electric bulb swinging slightly at the end of its flex, oscillated by the draughts that leaked into the place through a multitude of cracks, a woman past her menopause, freed at least from the inconvenience of babies. Did he have it in his heart to be sorry for her?

The handbag yielded nothing. He pulled the suitcase into the middle of the floor, its locks rusted beyond use and one of its clasps broken. The rubbish inside wasn't worth sending to a jumble sale but it represented the treasures of her lifetime, the only memories she had, cheap souvenirs of long-past holidays in popular resorts, a china ashtray, a man's pipe, its bowl charred, a broken string of artificial pearls, in a ring-case from which the cloth covering sloughed a ring more brass than gold. He glanced round at her and she had a sheen in her eyes but she was past tears, a long time ago. He riffled the pages of a twopenny notebook, their edges curling and blackened, mostly empty, only an address here and there, figures that perhaps represented telephone numbers, names which he took as those of ships, written in an unformed, childish hand, the last entry of all a house he knew in an avenue he knew in the town he'd left earlier that day.

He got up from his knees and sat on the edge of the bed, which creaked under his weight, a spring twanging with a musical note: "I'm a policeman."

"It doesn't show much."

The photograph lay on the table. "Until Ringer told me," the Sergeant said, "I didn't know who he was. I might never have found out."

"Was she as clever as that?"

"A friend of yours?"

A tired smile played about her lips and he hadn't believed she could smile: "She thought so."

"Hilda Smith?" he said, making a question of it.

"Not Smith, Blackoe."

"I didn't think it was." He spoke in a low voice. "What did she run away from?"

"Look at it," the woman said, gazing round the miserable attic.

"From him?"

"I'm getting old," she pitied herself. "He'd nothing about him but nobody else wanted me. I lived in a better place than this once and I was good enough for Todd till he found out she brought him more profit than I did."

"You knew where she'd gone? She wrote to you?"

"But I had to be careful if I wanted to get rid of her."

The Sergeant glanced at her doubtfully.

"In the end it was she who needed help," the woman told him.

"Why?"

"She had a husband."

"Had?"

"Has," and the woman smiled again.

"Go on!"

"It's only about a year since she started the game. Nothing to do, not much coming in." – she pulled a face – "I'm not blaming her but she shouldn't have tried to queer my pitch."

"Her husband?"

"A sailor on a tramp. He's not been home for eighteen months."

"Did he hear about it?"

"Somebody sent him a letter to tell him how she'd turned out," and the woman wasn't looking at him. She added, with her head lowered, "But he'd have known anyway."

"A baby she couldn't hide, even if he hadn't had a friend kind enough to put him right?"

"Does it show already?" She glanced at him with admiration. "You don't miss anything," and the coquetry returned to her manner, making her pathetic.

"You'd helped her to leave—"

"She wouldn't have come back but I'd had to pretend for too long I liked her. Things were working out for her and she was falling on her feet."

"She hadn't much scope," Cluff said, "if she was married already."

"Who knew? She'd a better deal in view. Being pregnant sent her off – Blackoe's no milksop – but she was even turning the baby to her advantage. If she played her cards right she could father it on the man she'd got a job with. It had only just started when she went."

The Sergeant sighed, remembering what Sally's brother had seen through the window, and Culter would have believed it perhaps. He'd never have got away and he'd have gone on believing it, consoling himself with tales of premature births. What mattered was how he saw her and no one could tell him she wasn't the embodiment of purity, a woman with a soul unsullied, fated for him. But would Hilda Blackoe know that or have a high enough opinion of men to trust that he'd defend her against the whole world?

"I've never had anything," the woman said sadly. "Why

should it happen to her – a home, money, somebody to love her? To be somebody, with a position, respect—"

"She did write to you," Cluff said. "Where she was, what she hoped for." He accused, "And you passed it on to Todd." He added, sadly, "You're worse off than before. You can't get him back now."

"Everything I do goes bad on me," she replied. "It always has. All I wanted was to get at her, for Todd to make her leave where she'd gone to—"

"By telling that she'd come off the streets?"

"I didn't know she'd kill him."

He didn't doubt her, and he could see it all, Todd using her, a man like that still a man, something to cling to until Hilda Blackoe came along and then her protector changing his allegiance, involving the younger woman, the prettier woman, deeper and deeper in the mire of human vice, the older property discarded, hopeless, with nothing left. He understood now how Todd had come to Gunnarshaw and why, the danger he was to the housekeeper, doubly so, not only because he knew what she'd been but because he knew she had a husband as well.

"Don't go!" and a withered hand, like a claw, extended to detain him. Her body brushed against his: he could smell her in his nostrils and read the invitation in her eyes. He sidled along the edge of the bed and it had to be true, but he couldn't leave it here. He needed to pile evidence on evidence, not for himself but for Bright, fact upon fact to support what he would have to say, to reinforce the picture he would have to draw, to reconcile the lover to the reality of his dream. He said, "She must have lived somewhere when her husband sailed.

She must have had people close to her. She can't have been entirely alone."

"Even if I give myself free," she thought, "he won't stay," and too much had happened to her, too many disappointments. She'd no fight in her and she knew her future. "A father," she answered, accepting. "Round the corner in the next street. At number six."

CHAPTER XII

The Sergeant didn't look round. Somehow he knew that she'd taken the place he'd vacated on the bed, that her neck couldn't support the weight of her head, that her greasy, stringy hair hung over her despairing eyes and the fingers of her hands in her lap twined and untwined on the vivid check of her skirt.

His feet clattered on the stairs. He passed landing after landing, their doors closed, the rooms they guarded silent, the naked butterfly flames of flaring gas-jets hardly relieving the noxious dark.

He forgot for a while the address he'd been given. He walked and the city was quiet, the hours in the attic longer than he'd imagined, the intervals long between question and answer, time slowed while he was there. The pubs had closed and the streets had cleared. An occasional figure slunk in an incipient fog rising from the river. The only sound was a distant rumble of cranes working through the night at a dock over the roofs.

He remembered his bag, which he'd left at the railway station, and he couldn't face a hotel, the lights of its hall, the signing of a register, the night porter showing him to a strange, unwelcoming room. He missed Clive at his heels and the outline of the moors in the sky.

He leaned on a railing, staring down at the black water lapping gently against the embankment. A ferry lay dark at a floating pier that rose and fell almost imperceptibly on the tide, cradled by the river: a white-painted liner, ablaze with light but its decks deserted, moored to a landing stage a little farther downstream: shipyards and buildings on the other side of the estuary rose in a confused, dim mass.

Salt on his lips tasted sharp on his tongue when he licked them and the wind from the sea whipped at his cheeks. He wanted to sail away too. Was he freer than the woman in the attic? Weren't they both trapped alike, she in her orbit and he in his?

He retraced his steps and passed again the door into which she'd taken him, turning a corner, straining his eyes at the numbers on the houses, looking for the one she'd told him. A light at least shone in its window, through a narrow gap between drawn curtains.

He stopped on the pavement and put his eye to the glass, his view barred by a grille of boards nailed clumsily from edge to edge of the frame inside. A man huddled in a chair by an empty grate, fully dressed, old and balding, his head trembling, his eyes darting.

The Sergeant knocked on the door, waiting in vain for an answer before he knocked again, more loudly and longer, with no greater success. The echoes of his blows died away and he listened for someone stirring inside the house but everything was quiet. He bent to the flap of a letter slot, rattling it and trying to peer through it, and all he could see was black dark in the passage.

He looked up and down the street and were these houses

of a back-to-back type, no entry except from the fronts? At the window again, the man in the room had straightened, sitting stiffly with eyes unblinking. He made not the slightest movement and gave no sign, not even the motion of breathing, that he was alive.

Cluff stayed a little longer, worried, by the door that was bolted and barred, by the planks nailed across the window, by the house in its state of siege. Nothing stirred in the street and still nothing moved in the room, either in the segment he could see or from the parts hidden from his sight. He doubted that the figure in the chair was human. An aura of fear accompanied him as he went away and where could he seek an explanation except in the one place he'd visited before?

He climbed back up the stairs as if this house had become a part of his life, something he'd never be free of. The unnatural silence both cowed him and demanded his own silence, making him tread lightly, halting him at each creak of the treads, compelling him to the shaky banister until the sound settled.

He stood like a statue in the doorway, hand on the handle, staring, bewildered, the room different, the hand-basin in fragments on the floor, the covers trailed from the bed, the chair overturned. Yet it wasn't the destruction he had eyes for but the woman, crumpled in a heap, her skirt rucked to her thighs, revealing tarnished flesh-pink lace round her legs.

He propped his stick against the wall and closed the door before he turned her on to her back. Her blouse had been ripped from neck to waist and he steeled himself to put a hand on her heart beneath her withered breast. Her jaw hung limply, reddened on one side, and the flesh about an eye puffed soggily, already beginning to discolour. A trickle of blood oozed from the corner of her mouth and ran slowly down her chin. His fingers traced a wan flutter and roved the skeleton of her fleshless body to make sure no bones were broken.

He lifted her on to the bed, covering her with one of its sheets. The ewer had escaped the general destruction and he wiped the blood away and bathed the bruises on her face. He righted the chair and sat beside her and little by little the oblong of the skylight paled. Her breathing, which when he arrived first had been unnoticeable, became stertorous and finally more normal. Her limbs under their covering twitched now and again and her head rolled on the pillow. She began to moan.

The lids of her eyes attempted to open, failed, tried again and then succeeded, but she shrank from him, the effort making her groan more. She lay still for a while, gathering what remained of her strength before she flung the sheet back with a sudden desperate movement and sat up. He pushed her down and she fought with him.

"Who was it?" Cluff asked, and the fear in her face was only too real. "Who?" he repeated, and she winced. "I'll go for the police," he said.

"No!" and this time he didn't restrain her. She swung her legs from the bed and pulled herself up, using him for a prop, gripping his lapels. "No!"

"Yes."

"I won't tell them anything."

He disengaged himself: "You're hurt."

"Would they be sorry? They know what I am."

"You've the same rights as other women."

She slipped to her knees, pressing herself against him, her arms like chains round his legs. "A man," she said urgently. "A man I picked up after you'd gone," and her voice was shrill. "It's nothing new. It'll happen again."

"Someday they'll kill you."

"No!" she repeated, and went on repeating it as he tried to get away. Her voice rose and full daylight seeped through the sooty skylight. "If you want it like that," he said, and what had he to do now with this city, enough of it already sticking in his craw? He turned at the door: "I went to her father's, or the house you told me was her father's. I couldn't get in. He was there but he wouldn't let me inside."

"Haven't you found out enough?"

"What are you frightened of?"

"Nothing," and her voice was shrill again. "Nothing! Nothing! Nothing! Todd's dead. She's not here. She's gone. I never want to see her again. She's caused me too much trouble."

"What have you caused her?" the Sergeant said, and went out.

Bristles sprouted on his jaw and cheeks and he felt dirty, both outside and in. He knew they were staring at him in the streets, the city waking, but the river drew him again. He watched the water, as he'd done last night, the ferry in service now, coasters out in midstream, a flow of taxis through the gates to the landing stage, where the liner had come to life, baggage nets soaring and plunging to its decks forward, white-coated stewards visible in its passenger accommodation, travellers beginning to cross from the shore on its gangways, a Blue Peter flying from its truck. An old man flung scraps to the gulls from a paper bag.

In the end he found a barber's shop and had himself shaved, maintaining a silence in the chair against the chatter of the assistant. He had to wait for a train when he'd rescued his bag from the left-luggage office but he was less conspicuous here. The woman in the buffet served him with tea and a sandwich, scarcely giving him a second glance. He drank the tea and left the sandwich uneaten.

CHAPTER XIII

In terms of actual distance his journey wasn't a long one but he had to change trains and time lengthened. The line of factories and houses bordering the track gave way gradually, first to market gardens and then to fields, and the flatter country began to swell into undulations and afterwards into hills. The bright promise of yesterday had failed to last and clouds massed to shut out the sun. A few drops of rain spattered the windows of his compartment but the weather didn't affect him either for better or worse.

"Let me take it," Barker said, as the Sergeant came out of the railway station at Gunnarshaw, and reached for his suitcase. Clive jumped at him in welcome and his stare at the car to which Barker led him was moody. He listened without comment to, "The Superintendent lent it to me. He told me to meet the trains. We guessed if you weren't on one you'd be on the other." Halfway to his cottage he said, "I didn't say where I was going."

"I was with you in the café," Barker answered, without taking his attention from his driving. "I knew as well as Mole the postmark on the letters. The Chief Superintendent traced you on the telephone," and he concentrated on the road, not entirely happy to be in charge of a car that didn't belong to him, the more so in view of its owner.

Annie took the case as they entered the cottage, holding her tongue with an effort, disappearing up the stairs. The dog and Barker came into the living-room behind him and Chief Superintendent Patterson got to his feet, carefully placing Jenet from his lap on to the cushions. "You've moved in?" the Sergeant asked.

"I'd like to."

"Aren't I doing my job properly?"

"I'd a yearning for the country," the Superintendent explained, as he'd done already to Mole and Barker at the police station. "This was a good excuse."

"You must have set off early."

"I came yesterday afternoon. I decided to spend the night in Gunnarshaw."

Cluff reached for his pipe and tobacco from the mantel. He moved the cat and sat down, slow in completing his preparation for a smoke. Annie Croft came in with a tray of cutlery and crockery and began to set the table, noisily, her temper strained. She managed to refrain from comment for a while and then she burst out, "He's never had his suitcase open: he didn't go to bed last night." She added, after a moment's struggle with herself, "And I'll bet he hasn't had a bite since he went away."

"I'm fat enough," Cluff objected.

Patterson let her leave the room for the kitchen: "It didn't take you long."

"Alphonsus Todd," the Sergeant replied. "A ponce. Bright Culter's housekeeper was one of his women. She's married, she's going to have a child, she's changed her name. She's got her eye on Bright and he's probably too far gone on her to save. The child hasn't been conceived long: he'll know no better if she says it's his."

Annie returned to the table, carrying a large meat and potato pie: "Come and get it."

"I'm not hungry," the Sergeant said.

"You weren't asked," and she didn't retire to the kitchen until the three of them were seated with knives and forks in their hands.

Patterson remarked with his mouth full, "This by itself was worth coming to Gunnarshaw for." Barker bent his head over his plate, occasionally glancing surreptitiously at Cluff, not enjoying his food very much. The cat slept and Clive was too well-trained to leave the hearthrug.

The Sergeant toyed with his meal: "Don't you want to know?"

The Superintendent went on eating. He cleared the first plateful and helped himself to a second from the dish.

"She killed him," Cluff said.

"It had to be someone nearby," the Superintendent answered.

"Mole thought so as well."

"Preferably not from Gunnarshaw," Patterson added.

"She made one mistake. She told the woman who'd helped her to get away where she was."

"The letters!" Barker interrupted.

"She had them all right." Cluff put his knife and fork down with a clatter. "Once Todd got to know it was all up with her if he opened his mouth."

"Blackmail?"

"Culter wouldn't have appreciated the truth. He might

have thought he loved her – perhaps he'd even reason to think the child was his. But he'd have jibbed at bigamy if nothing else. She'd the legal husband in the background."

"Reason enough. What was Bright doing while this was going on?"

"Sitting in the pictures watching cowboys and Indians, or on the road home at any rate."

The Sergeant got up and went back to his chair. Annie came in with an apple tart and opened her mouth only to close it with a snap when Patterson shook his head at her warningly. The Superintendent finished his meal and so did Barker and the two of them moved to the fire as well, Patterson opposite Cluff and the detective-constable on the couch. Annie served them cups of tea in their hands. The Sergeant told her, "You're behind your time again."

"You've got guests."

"I'm going," Patterson said. "They'll think at Headquarters they've lost me for good." He finished his tea without hurrying and lit his own pipe and toasted his feet for a while at the fire before getting up and stretching. "I don't want to, Caleb, but there's nothing else for it. You're a lucky man."

"With what I've got to do?"

"I meant this," and the Superintendent waved in a gesture that took in the cottage. "Barker can arrest her – or Mole. It'd please the Inspector." His pipe had gone out and he put a match to it. "Culter'll realize someday what a lucky escape he's had."

"You're leaving it to me."

"She won't run away. You can choose your own time."

"With him there – or without him?"

The Superintendent's look told Barker to stay where he was and he said from the doorway, "Put it in writing, Caleb, when you feel like it: I've got to keep the Chief Constable happy."

They listened to Patterson's car driving off and Annie came in for the cups. Her eyes met Barker's and, satisfied that he wasn't going to leave too, she said, "I'll be off when I've done the washing-up."

The fire crackled and the lids began to droop over Barker's eyes. He sat up with a jerk: "A warrant?"

"I'll take her to the station first." The Sergeant looked into the fire. "You'd better give Mole a ring. We have to live with him. He's capable of sticking his oar in if he thinks we're too long about it. We don't want him going after Bright."

He could hear Barker on the telephone in the passage and he was going over it again, to make absolutely certain, but it couldn't have been anybody else. "He can't believe it," Barker said, returning and sitting down in the chair Patterson had used. The cat got tired of Cluff and came across to him and the daylight faded but they'd nothing to do that needed light and he preferred not to see the Sergeant's face too clearly.

If they'd both been asleep Mole's entrance would have wakened them. The Inspector came in with a rush, accompanied by a blast of cold air, leaving the doors open behind him. In spite of the chill outside his face was flushed and he looked hot under the collar. Barker gave him the gist of the story as he'd heard it from Cluff, solicitous to leave out what they'd learnt in the cottage belonging to Sally two nights ago.

Mole pulled at the knot of his tie and he didn't like it,

remembering his own tip in the murder stakes. The fact that caution had prevented him from pressing the point with Patterson in the police station yesterday afternoon gave him some consolation, but not when he faced the Sergeant. He admitted that the letters could have been from the woman with whom Cluff had talked in the attic, or from Todd, but that Culter had handed them over unopened was a difficult pill to swallow. He wanted to stick to his previous objection that a knife wasn't a woman's weapon but, if he did, he'd only be told there were women and women.

Barker began to get restive. The fire had gone down and it was so dark by now in the living-room they could hardly see each other, and parky too. The Inspector didn't leave and sooner or later Cluff must. Thinking back, the detective-constable seemed to recall dimly the faint wail of the five o'clock buzz in Gunnarshaw, audible here when the wind blew in the right direction.

"I've got my car," Mole said.

The Sergeant told him, "I'm taking the dog."

"On an occasion like this?"

"I had to leave him yesterday."

"Very well."

Barker mended the fire before they left and none of them said anything in the car. Even at the Inspector's speed they did the trip in five minutes or so, drawing up by the entrance to Culter's. The Sergeant got out and stared hard at Mole's house, from the kitchen window of which a light shone, but the Inspector wouldn't take the hint. It was dark at the weaver's and the gate, not properly shut, swung in the wind, its hinges creaking. Mole stepped between the Sergeant and

Barker and they all went up the drive, Clive as well.

The back door was shut but the inner door leading directly into the kitchen ajar. The blind must have fitted well because the room had a light in it but Mole gave a nervous cough and a switch clicked, extinguishing the light abruptly. They halted, crowding the small enclosed vestibule, and the hairs on the nape of Barker's neck pricked.

Cluff pushed the inner door open and the exact sequence of events wasn't clear but somebody switched the light on again and Barker gasped. In one way their journey had been wasted but in another they'd arrived at exactly the right moment. Did he feel a little surge of relief that the Sergeant, after all, wouldn't have to carry the responsibility of taking Hilda Blackoe from the man who'd fallen in love with her?

She lay full length on the floor, between the table and the hearth, just as dead as Todd had been but much bloodier, the blouse she wore stained crimson, a pool of blood spreading near her left breast. A man Barker had never seen before, a tall, strong ox of a man with a barrel chest and sturdy, bowed legs, thick arms whose muscles bulged through his sleeves, stood by her, gazing at them. He had a thin-bladed knife in his fingers and the blue tattoo of an anchor on the back of his hand had changed to red.

Cluff jumped suddenly to one side and Mole to the other. The knife came whizzing through the air between them and buried itself quivering in the wood of the jamb, a few inches from Barker's ear. The dog shot past him, fangs bared, and attacked, sending the stranger staggering, but he got a grip on its collar and hurled it at the Sergeant, who stumbled back into Mole. Barker saw the man diving for a door on the other side of the kitchen and he didn't wait, turning and running outside as fast as he could, along the gable end. Mole's wife, at her door on the other side of the fence, shouted and a car passing along the avenue stopped with a screech of brakes. Doors in other houses opened and voices added their quota to the disturbance flowering in this quiet, correct residential area. He swerved round the corner as the big man emerged from the front door with his fists up and a look on his face that boded no good for anyone.

Barker went for his legs in a rugby tackle. They hit the hard macadam of the path with a crash that jarred his bones but he held on in spite of flailing feet. A short bank dropped to the lawn at a lower level and they rolled down it together, clutching at each other. Hands groped for his neck and then thumbs for his eyes and he jerked his head wildly but he didn't release his grip. He could feel the wet of the grass and the soft ground giving under their weight.

He didn't believe he could last much longer and then he was on his feet and someone was saying, "Let go!" Men closed in over the narrow flowerbed dividing the drive from the lawn and pushed through the low hedge separating Culter's from its neighbour in the same block. Women lining the pavement on the other side of the outer wall tried ineffectively to shoo their children away: infants screamed: car horns hooted: the feet of late-comers rattled on the road. His face heavy with strain, panting, Cluff exerted his strength to lever the man loose from Barker and Clive tugged at a trouser leg, his teeth buried in the cloth. Mole danced attendance, blowing piercingly on a whistle stuck between his lips.

They had him now, sheer numbers too much for him,

the citizens of Gunnarshaw rallying in support, and he was mumbling but if anyone heard nobody listened and he quietened, abandoning his struggle. The police car for which Mrs Mole had phoned ejected a quartette of constables, who charged unnecessarily through the spectators, hurling them aside. Completely passive by this time their prisoner could have been led away by one of the excited children but they came in useful, at least, to disperse the crowd. Heads wagged, nothing like this in Gunnarshaw, not in this district anyway, since it had been green fields: they'd all expected it, of course, and that it had occurred at Culter's house was inevitable.

Barker, wincing from the kicks and blows he'd taken, brushed the mud of the lawn as best he could from his clothes and realized suddenly that Culter wasn't there. Cluff must have realized it too, and Mole, because they weren't in the garden any more and lights were going on in the windows all over the house. The police drove away with their captive and he darted for the front door, his heart beating faster.

A subdued Mole descended the stairs slowly and Cluff came out of the sitting-room. They looked at each other and both of them shook their heads. "Go across to the Inspector's," the Sergeant told Barker, "and get hold of Hamm. When you've done that see if anybody's still in at the mill. Bright ought to have been home by now."

Barker made his telephone calls. Coming back up the drive he saw Cluff by the shed at the end of the garden, with his face pressed to the window, through which the workbench, with its vice and its lathe and grindstone, and the rack of tools, could be just made out. "He's not there either," the Sergeant said, fingering a lock fastening a hasp and staple on the door. He added, "He went in for woodwork, how seriously I'm not sure but it'd get him away from the house in his mother's time."

Barker almost asked, "Have you looked over the hedge?" but Hamm's car drew up in the road and they went to meet him. The surgeon whistled when he saw Hilda Blackoe's body and remarked, "Once it begins it goes on. What's the old saying – events happen in threes?" He smiled grimly. "There's one thing, you're more than halfway there."

The Inspector pulled the knife from the door jamb, very cautiously, with a handkerchief wrapped round it and held it out for inspection: "We came to arrest her. Two minutes earlier and we'd have caught him in the act."

"Never mind," the surgeon replied. "You've still got my congratulations. I couldn't have arranged it better myself." He reached for the knife but Mole withdrew it hastily to prevent him from touching it. "That's the one anyway," Hamm said a little later. "It fits your other victim too, only she died from it and he didn't."

"It wasn't for want of her trying," Cluff said, and the surgeon cocked his head.

"That's why you came for her? She killed that man in Rigsby's garden?" and Hamm read the answer in the Sergeant's face. "Neat," he said. "Very neat. There's a phrase for it—"

"Poetic justice."

"Any kind of justice. Where's Culter?" No one answered him. He went on, "You know, if I was a member of a Trade Union I'd go on strike. You're overworking me. I shan't know whether or not to go to bed tonight. It won't be worth it if you're going to call me out again as soon as I get tucked up."

CHAPTER XIV

The Sergeant sat behind his table in the C.I.D. room, slouching in the chair, tweed-trousered legs and muddy boots extended, almost touching Clive lying on the floor. He hid his hands in the pockets of his unbuttoned Burberry: his head inclined forward and his chin rested on his chest. He'd pushed back his disreputable tweed hat and his eyes were red and bloodshot from lack of sleep. The room, with its painted walls and its board floor, lit by the bulb under the white, plate-like shade, looked very cold and bare and dusty.

Inspector Mole came in from the outer office: "No one's seen him since he left the mill at five. I've ordered every man out in the town to look for him."

Cluff got to his feet and walked to the door. "Harry," he called to the Duty Constable, and nodded at the mouth of the corridor leading to the cells at the back of the station. The tramp of the constable's feet across the floor drowned the sound of his own return to his chair. "Culter's had it," the Inspector said, and couldn't decide, from a purely personal point of view, how much regret to express.

The Duty Constable reappeared, escorting the big man they'd found standing over Hilda Blackoe. He had a surly expression on his face, a despairing obstinacy in his manner, his eyes dull, his body slack. Ink from a pad stained the ends of his thick fingers but he'd washed the blood off his hands and the tattoo stood out more clearly. They'd taken his jacket away and he wore a sleeveless pullover, with his shirtsleeves rolled up. Snakes crawled up his forearms, slithering on his skin when he moved. He glanced over his shoulder as Barker came in too, with the knife and white cards marked with sets of fingerprints, staying near the door with the Duty Constable. They all waited for Cluff to speak and the silence seemed eternal.

"Blackoe!" the Sergeant said suddenly, but the prisoner stayed still, not a muscle of his face flickering. Inspector Mole started, the pace too rapid for him, Cluff too much in command, too knowledgeable.

"We might have met last night," the Inspector heard. "You couldn't have been gone long when I went back to that attic a second time."

"Sergeant—" Barker began, but the look he received in reply didn't encourage him to continue.

"Why did you beat that prostitute up?" Cluff asked. "Everything she'd written to you was true. She'd have told you where your wife was without that." He got no reply to his question and answered it with another. "Simply because she'd written to you, telling you what you'd probably suspected but didn't want proving? You must have had some idea of what your wife was, that without you she wouldn't sit quietly by the fireside. I'd been to her father's and he knew you. He hadn't barred his door and nailed up his windows for nothing. They're all afraid of you. How many times, I wonder, have you threatened to do your wife in, to the crew you sailed with, to everyone you met as soon as you made port at the end of your voyage? When was that – yesterday, the day before?"

His shot went home. It wounded but it didn't infuriate this bull of a man. More and more he deflated, cowed into a wondering docility, like an animal beaten remorselessly, its spirit broken, hurt more in its feelings than in its flesh, unable to understand its faults.

"That woman," Cluff said, "whose place with Todd your wife took, who wrote to you about her – you knew where to start your search. You'd no doubts left and your wife hadn't any illusions she could convince you people had lied about her. She'd got herself pregnant and perhaps she hadn't the courage to try to get rid of it or perhaps she'd had enough of you anyway. But it wasn't Todd she was running away from, it was you." His head came up and he looked Blackoe full in the face. "You've been in trouble before," and it wasn't a question this time. "It won't be hard to find out that it's violence you were guilty of."

"Sergeant—" Barker attempted a second time, and got no farther than he had done before.

"She wasn't worth it," Cluff said. "Look what you've done to yourself. You'd have killed her anyway, with your bare hands if the knife hadn't been there for you to snatch. It wouldn't have meant a hanging by itself – but Culter too. What have you done with him?" The minutes passed and the Sergeant shrugged. "He couldn't help himself any more than you could. She twisted him round her little finger as she did you when you married her. Why didn't you let the blame remain where it lay?"

They all thought Blackoe was going to speak at last but the moment passed. The Inspector said, "What's the use? You were there with the knife in your fingers and blood on your hands. Tell us the rest of it." The prisoner's eyes turned to him, making him back a pace before their fire died away.

"You've got it all worked out," the sailor said.

"It isn't up to me," Cluff told him. "I'd do my best for you, but I'm not the judge."

"She had an allotment," Blackoe said. "She didn't need to go on the streets," and was he speaking to them or to himself? If he'd been a smaller man, Barker thought, he wouldn't have roused so much sympathy but his size made him the more defenceless. His head didn't match the proportions of his body: his face was battered and crushed, strength not intelligence his only weapon and strength wouldn't serve him now. He couldn't fight his bewilderment with his fists or calculate an escape from the pit he'd dug for himself, the trap into which he'd fallen. A faint odour of alcohol still clung to his breath. Had he been aware of what he was doing? When he saw her lying dead at his feet could he realize, at that moment, how it had come about?

"Haven't you anything else to say?" Cluff pleaded.

His features mirrored the rusty working of his mind, the grinding out of half-formed ideas, too puerile and imperfect to merit expression. He couldn't think and he'd never thought, only acted. The effort was too much for him, ceasing almost as soon as it started: words wouldn't help him even if he'd had words and that, at least, registered in what he had of a brain. His acceptance, his defeat, the impossibility of concocting any excuse, were visible. Had he really loved her, Barker wondered? Now that she didn't exist was there anything more left for him than there would have been for Culter?

The telephone on Cluff's table rang shrilly. He let it ring and they watched him, listening. He made a little gesture at the Duty Constable but even when Blackoe had gone something of his presence still remained in the room.

The Inspector moved to the table and picked up the receiver. He handed it to Cluff, who put it to his ear, Patterson's voice weakly audible from the other end of the line. The Sergeant said slowly, "I didn't have to. Her husband got there first. He'd killed her." When Barker looked again the receiver was back on its rest, the Sergeant huddled in his chair, Mole immobile, the dog under the table staring into infinity. He glanced down at his hands and dropped the knife on the table top and put the finger-print cards beside it. A dryness gagged his throat and he said what he'd tried to say twice already, "His prints are there but the knife's got others, underneath, smudged, not clear—"

"It's hers," Cluff interrupted, and the knife had started life as an ordinary article of cutlery, its bone handle smooth, but someone had ground its blade to a razor-edge, into a needle-like sharpness.

"What do we need the fingerprints for? He doesn't deny it," the Inspector said. "How could he?" and Clive came from under the table to follow Cluff to the door. "You'll be at home?" Mole called after him. "I'll ring you as soon as there's any news about Culter."

Barker, too, went into the outer office and no one told him to stay or gave him any orders. He picked up his hat and coat from where he'd left them on the public counter and joined Cluff and Clive in the street. They made their way across the town, taking the road past Culter's house, where a uniformed

constable at the gate shook his head as they went by. The
street-lamps ended at the junction of the avenue with the
direct route from the centre of Gunnarshaw and they went on
into the night.

"I waited," Cluff said. "I'd known from the moment I first
talked with her she must have killed Todd. When I came back
this morning I knew why, what there'd been at stake for her,
that he could have ruined all her plans. I could have gone for
her then."

"You couldn't have imagined her husband would follow
her."

"I waited," the Sergeant repeated. "I let the whole day go
by. She's dead too, and perhaps Bright. It could end like that
for Blackoe!"

Now that their eyes grew accustomed to the dark the night
seemed less black. Somewhere behind the clouds a moon
diffused a wan light.

"My fault," Cluff said. "There wasn't any way in which I
could have shielded Bright from the facts he had to know.
What did I hope to accomplish by putting it off?"

The hedges unrolled on either side of them and Barker
stopped, not sure whether his eyes deceived him, a movement
on the slope to their right, a shadow lurching and weaving
in an aimless progress, wandering, getting nowhere. He put a
hand on Cluff's sleeve and then pointed. The shapeless form
drifted this way and that until it collided with a fence and
paused before it climbed the rails, outlined against the sky. It
had legs and a body and its foot caught, sending it toppling
forward out of view.

They ran. Scratches on Barker's face and hands smarted

where the thorns had torn at him as they forced a path through the roadside hedge. His feet skidded in the grass and the dog jumping about his legs hindered his progress. He leapt the fence ahead of Cluff and a long, low, stone-built shed materialized in front of him, its walls crumbling, roofed only by a mesh of rafters from which a gale in the past had riven their tarred sheets of corrugated iron, leaving the stalls beneath exposed to the weather. The Sergeant pulled up at his side and they listened to the sound of someone sobbing. They splashed through the mud churned up by cattle and sheep where a trough had overflowed and a man broken, destroyed, surrendering pride and will, all dignity spurned, crouched in a corner, under the remains of a manger.

The match Cluff had struck went out and Barker remembered the torch he carried in his pocket. He flashed the beam on to Bright Culter, who lifted his face to them, his eyes closed as if he was praying. The Sergeant lifted him gently to his feet and he leaned, exhausted, against the rough, undressed stone of the wall, the pressure of his body dislodging fragments of mortar.

"How did you find out?" Cluff asked.

"I wanted her to marry me," Culter moaned.

"What she was," the Sergeant finished his question, "that she could never marry you?"

"She was going to have a child."

"Yours?"

"It couldn't be mine."

"No," Cluff said. "Even though you lived in the same house with her. I should never have let myself doubt that for a moment. Didn't you realize how much she wanted to get you into bed?" Culter's eyes opened wider, round and staring, different without the spectacles he'd lost in his flight. "Did you quarrel?" the Sergeant continued. "It's not so hard now: I can tell you she's dead." He saw Culter, in the light of Barker's torch, start to slide down the wall, his knees buckling, and he grabbed him to hold him up. "On top of everything else she's committed murder. That man in the garden – he could have told you about her. She had to silence him or pay his price. Didn't you guess? Could it have been anyone but her?"

Culter swallowed and his mouth worked. He stammered, "I couldn't stay there. I had to get away."

"You've been luckier than you know. We thought he'd killed you too." He couldn't read the emotions in the other's face before Barker lowered his torch a little. "Her husband," he said, "but not because of you. Because of what she's been and what she'd done before she came to you."

Culter's fingers scrabbled at the wall behind him and his body was a dead weight in Cluff's grip. He said, "Her husband?"

"Didn't you know she had one?"

"I'd begun to suspect."

"And taxed her with it?"

"When I got home this afternoon – with that – and with the baby." He repeated, "I couldn't stay with her, not after what she said. I had to get away."

"He must have come just after you'd gone. He hasn't tried to clear himself. It would be useless if he did. We caught him there, with the knife in his hands." He urged Barker, "Help me," as Culter collapsed bonelessly, chalk-white, in a faint.

He held the weaver against one leg, kneeling on the other, and bathed his face with a handkerchief Barker had moistened in the trough. He heard, after a while, "She'd kept being sick in the mornings," and Culter's voice trailed away. "I wasn't ever going to see her again. I couldn't have faced her."

"It's all over."

"I knew in my heart—"

"You were out that night. At the pictures."

"She wouldn't come with me. She persuaded me to go."

"She'd arranged for a visitor."

"I wanted to kill myself: I was going to kill myself."

"Blackoe's a big man. If you'd been there you couldn't have saved her."

"Would I have tried after what she'd taunted me with?"

"You couldn't have stood by and watched him drive the knife into her heart."

"She's still there?"

"Not now. Will you go back?"

"I can't."

"Come home with me. For tonight." The Sergeant got to his feet and took Barker aside. "Tell Mole. Do what you can to get the kitchen cleaned up."

CHAPTER XV

"He what?" the Inspector exclaimed.

"He ran away."

"It was his house, not hers."

"The bottom had dropped out of his world. The Sergeant believes him."

"No one else would have taken so long to see what her game was." The Inspector glanced at Barker. "Don't you?"

"Believe him?"

"What else?"

"It's in character."

"Another man," the Inspector affirmed, "would have killed her there and then, saving her husband a job."

"It's fortunate we caught sight of him in the fields."

"Pass the word," Mole told the Duty Constable. "The search is off." He asked Barker, "He's gone home?"

"The Sergeant's taken him to the cottage."

"And I'm expected to keep a man on his house until he consents to come back to lock his door?"

"I'm just going there. Culter gave me his key."

The Inspector drove him from the police station and the constable left on guard wasn't at the gate but they found him by the toolshed with the reflector of his torch against the glass of the window. "You'll have to break in," Mole remarked, making him jump. "As long as I've lived here that shed's been kept locked. Even when his mother was living he allowed nobody to set a foot over the threshold."

"There's some good stuff in there," the constable replied. "I haven't got tools like that."

"We'll know where to look if anything's missing. Get off duty!"

"The house?"

"It won't sprout wings and fly. Barker's going to lock up."

"What's happened?"

"Culter went for a walk."

"Well," the constable said, "he couldn't have picked a better time for an outing," and the Inspector shepherded him to the gate, where they parted, Mole to his own house, the policeman for the town.

Barker went into Culter's kitchen and they'd taken her to the mortuary, nothing to be seen but the pool of blood on the coconut matting and a slight disarrangement of the furniture. He supposed Cluff knew the people of Gunnarshaw more intimately than he did and if Blackoe hadn't admitted it in words his attempt to escape, his silence, the knife in his hand, had done it for him. He didn't need to shout his guilt from the rooftops. The detective-constable found a bucket and a cloth and began to clean up the blood: it fitted, it all fitted, right from the start, and he ought to have been happy, too, at this conclusion but that had been fear on Bright Culter's face in the field when they came on him.

He'd no right to stay in this house but he didn't want to leave. He preferred the violence of Blackoe to the feminine

weakness of its owner and he could see with Cluff that Culter
hadn't had much of a chance, but the result wasn't pretty.
Without his glasses his eyes were shifty: he was too soft and
flabby, as if he'd over-indulged in what harmless pleasures he'd
been allowed. When Barker thought of the sailor in his cell
local patriotism lost its appeal and the knife bothered him,
those other smudged prints on its handle. She could have used
it to try to protect herself but she'd been a fool to keep it after
Todd's death and he couldn't believe she'd ever been a fool.
If he could have bought one like it in a shop he'd have been
satisfied but it was too home-made and how much time and
care and skill had been required to convert it from its original
purpose?

He opened a drawer in the table, divided into compartments
lined with green baize. Not to have found table knives at all
would have been wrong and these had bone handles but so
had the knives, probably, in half the houses in the town.
Nevertheless, he locked the back door on the inside and went
into the passage by the stairs without turning on the light,
crossing the living-room to draw the curtains. As he pulled
them to, the moon illuminated the hedge at the bottom of the
lawn, the gardens beyond, the bulk of Rigsby's house and of its
neighbours. The stones in the rockery looked very white and
did Cluff believe she'd killed Todd there before putting him
over the hedge? The letters, he thought, and they'd prove she
told him to come and when, and she'd have had time, with
Culter out all day, to grind down the knife on the wheel in
the shed, getting its key in some way into her possession. But
if the men in these houses went to work the women stayed at
home and how much noise would the wheel make or where

had she learnt to use it? The Inspector's wife had a clothes-line immediately over the fence on to which the shed backed, people looked out of windows while doing their household chores – if he asked would he be told of a disposition on the part of Hilda Blackoe to spend her time in her employer's workshop?

Barker made certain the curtains overlapped, without a gap through which a Peeping Tom could peer, and had that youth imagined more than he'd seen or seen less than there actually was between Culter and his housekeeper? He'd loved her and wanted to marry her and when he'd found out the truth he wouldn't have killed her, not her, himself rather. Killed her! The detective-constable pulled himself up with a jerk. What was he trying to do, destroy the obvious, argue against the Sergeant, damage the reputation of Gunnarshaw by casting doubts on the innocence of its citizens when there were culprits readymade from another community? Facts didn't lie, her connection with Todd, her flight from her husband's vengeance, Blackoe's return from sea.

He shivered, sweat cold on his forehead, and put on the lights. The room closed in on him, heavy, forbidding, colourless, its furniture smelling of age, brought here perhaps from those rooms above Fred's café where old Mrs Culter had once lived. If walls had ears and could talk! Was he growing too much like Cluff? Had this concern with atmosphere, with people not with actions, rubbed off on to him during their association? They couldn't both be right and he was the tyro but Culter meant nothing to him and he'd hardly known the man.

The letters! His mind kept coming back to the letters and

she'd kept the knife – couldn't she have kept the letters as well? He used his torch now instead of the house-lights and he felt like a criminal, creeping upstairs with his heart in his mouth, not bold enough for a thief.

Articles of clothing draped the chairs in her bedroom: stockings hung from the frame of the mirror on the dressing-table over pots of face-creams and cosmetics: a transparent, flimsy nightdress lay on the bed. Her drawers were mostly empty, only two or three dresses and a coat in the wardrobe. A cheap suitcase contained nothing personal to connect her with her past and he was chasing shadows, worse, not knowing why he was chasing them.

A single bed, provided with a hard mattress, occupied the room Culter slept in and what was he looking for here? Methodically, in the dark, with the curtains drawn as an additional precaution to conceal the beam of his torch, Barker went through Culter's possessions as he had done those of the dead woman.

For a long time afterwards he sat on the floor, cross-legged, with the torch switched off, wishing that he'd left well alone.

CHAPTER XVI

His feet stubbed one of the stones bordering the garden path and he heard Clive barking. The room behind the dormer window was lit and so was the living-room.

The front door opened, blocked by the Sergeant's form, and the dog advanced growling before coming forward in welcome. "Who's there?" Cluff demanded.

"Barker," and he saw the light in the bedroom go out.

He left his hat and coat in the passage and the couch in the living-room was made up as a bed with pillow and sheets. Jenet slept in the seat of the armchair and the Sergeant had his slippers on, his shirt-neck open, his collar and tie on the mantelpiece. A red eye of fire winked in the grate.

"She didn't kill Todd," Barker said.

"She killed him."

"No!"

"Sit down." The Sergeant moved the sheets and the pillow to one end of the couch and went back to the passage door and shut it. Before he took the letters Barker held out miserably he filled and lit his pipe. "Where did you get them?" he said, after he'd read them.

"At Culter's house."

"You frightened me. They prove my point."

"Except that they were locked away, hidden, in Culter's

room not hers." He watched Cluff's face. "He never gave them to her after all." He added, "One or two from the woman you saw but mostly from Todd and those tell their own story."

"It isn't possible!"

"Todd's are the important ones, though Culter's probably still watching for more from the woman, the first saying he'd found out where she was."

"What reason was there to intercept it?"

"None – or curiosity? An accident, perhaps, when Culter and the postman met on the original occasion. He wanted her then: he'd given her work. But what could she have told him? Oughtn't he to have asked for references from the women who answered his advertisement, for some logical account of their qualifications, where they'd worked before, what she was doing in Gunnarshaw? Her appearance got her the job but was he entirely satisfied?"

"It's supposition."

"It's happened," Barker said. "Todd's second letter, complaining that the housekeeper hadn't replied to the first, and Culter expected it. A third, in stronger terms, asking for money, threatening to tell what he knew about her: a fourth to say he'd visited Gunnarshaw and discovered where the house was: a fifth and last about a meeting he thought she wouldn't dare to miss, on the night he was killed, in the shed he'd seen, to which he couldn't have known she'd no access."

"No access?"

"Culter never let anyone in there. Mole knows."

"It doesn't follow."

"Didn't you believe he'd never had anything in his life before, that he'd never been so close to love?"

"But what the letters don't say about her he must have read between the lines."

"Did he really accept what was implied in them; had he any thought but to protect her? But others, who didn't love her, would have had no scruples. How did his neighbours treat him because he was below them in the social scale? They'd have had a finer time with her."

"What else?"

"The knife. He has a grindstone in the shed."

"He was at the cinema," but there was no force in the Sergeant's objection.

"Did he stay to the end of the programme? There's an exit at the back, past the gentlemen's lavatory."

"Hilda Blackoe was in the house."

"It was raining. In any case, she wouldn't be wandering in the garden at that time and Sally's brother had been about, the curtains would be drawn close. Culter was keeping the appointment meant for her. She knew nothing about it and it was a wet, windy night." He noticed Clive's head turn to the closed door of the room. "Did you hear something?" He relaxed, the wind whistling as it had done that night, making the trees in the orchard creak, the cottage itself vocal, grumbling, continually flexing its joints.

"Todd died from the blow on his skull," Cluff said.

"Culter might never have spoken to him. A stone from the rockery flung to stun him as he turned – if his skull was exceptionally thin Culter didn't know. He couldn't be sure that the man was dead when he fell."

Cluff's voice was sad: "Then he intended to kill him?"

"Maybe not. The knife for protection, but when he saw

Todd standing there he couldn't resist. The stone back on the rockery, where the rain washed it clean, the railway ticket taken from his pocket, Todd tipped over the hedge into Rigsby's garden, a small man who didn't weigh much, easier for Culter, though, than for the housekeeper."

"And I live alone too," the Sergeant murmured.

"There's no comparison. You know everybody. Everybody talks to you. You've got Clive and Jenet, this cottage, your books. It's your own choice, it wasn't his—"

Cluff didn't hear him. He asked, "Is that why I felt for him? I could see why he wanted her. I could see what she was if his eyes were closed. I could understand what it would do to him if he lost her. I could forgive him for loving her." The eye of the fire had dimmed and the wind blew louder. "He'd dreamed and it was up to me."

Barker said remorselessly, "It was his knife. She died by it too."

"He loved her."

"He ran away."

"Because they'd quarrelled and he couldn't bear to be with her."

"When did he say it?"

"When?"

"After you'd told him her husband killed her."

"Not a second time!"

"I couldn't make them out, those blurred prints under Blackoe's on the handle of the knife but the smudges were too large for a woman's."

The Sergeant pushed himself to his feet with his hands on the arms of his chair. He took a step or two for the door and stopped. Barker, calling Clive to him, stayed where he was, stroking the dog's head as it rested on his thigh.

A latch clicked and he both heard and felt the inrush of icy wind. He jumped to his feet, past Cluff, into the passage, where the lamp had been blown out, no faintest glow on the landing at the head of the dark stairs, as black up there as the night into which he looked through the open front door.

"He saw me come," Barker said. "He was listening."

"I don't know him. I never knew him," the Sergeant replied.

"He's gone."

"Who do I know?" and Cluff's face twisted. "After this, who can I ever know?"

CHAPTER XVII

Blackoe hunched on the edge of the bed in the detention cell at the police station, bigger than Cluff, who leaned against the bare wall. "You're not dumb," the Sergeant said, and Barker, who'd just arrived in the doorway, could catch no hint either of complaint or of reproach in his tone.

"I didn't come here to take her back," Blackoe told him.

The bed, the lavatory basin at its foot, the washbasin facing the door, the small wooden table and chair, hardly left space for the two of them. An unshaded bulb hung high from the whitewashed ceiling, bringing into relief the iron grille inset over the square window on a level with it.

"You could live for thirty years yet."

"I've lived for over forty."

"Is that long enough?"

The sailor's brown skin, weathered by salt and wind, deepened the blue of his clear eyes. Something of the innocence of a child still clung to him and Barker sensed a similar remoteness in the Sergeant, as if both men had got lost in urban living, people, unless of their own kind, too much for them, their destined spheres the wide spaces, the free, endless vistas, one of the sea, the other of the land, but each simple and obstinate and unyielding.

"They won't hang you, not now," Cluff said.

"You've changed your tune."

"It's only your wife. The man she worked for's still alive."

"You thought he was dead, not me."

"This helps no one."

"She was mine."

"She'd been yours."

"It had to be finished. Would you have let her get away with it?"

"They'll shut you up, in a cell like this. It'll go on for months, perhaps years."

"You won't suffer."

"You didn't kill her."

Blackoe laughed: "You saw me there."

"Still—"

"No one'll listen to you. They'll be glad if I go to hell my own way."

"It's been some time since that woman wrote to you about your wife."

"She didn't let the grass grow under her feet." He showed his teeth. "I hadn't been away six months."

"You could have come back."

"I'd signed articles. I'd a living to earn, mine as well as hers."

"And you'd a year to think about it, on the other side of the world, no more letters, no news, only your imagination to tell you what was happening or what wasn't happening."

"You called at her father's, didn't you say? He knew what I'd do to him to find her. That woman told me – you know what I did to her."

"You couldn't stop yourself."

"Then why should I stop myself in Gunnarshaw?"

The Sergeant turned on his heel, forcing both Barker and Clive in the corridor to step quickly out of his path. In the public office the nightman on the counter said, "Nothing. We'll get nowhere till it's daylight."

Cluff went into his room and sat in his chair behind the table: "Culter's got to be found." Barker tried to reassure him: "We're doing everything we can."

"I have to get it out of him." The Sergeant's fingers clenched into a fist and he smashed his hand on the table top. "Don't you see what's at stake? I've blundered enough."

"You're not responsible for Blackoe."

"I gave the time to her murderer. Right or wrong I could have had her in the cell he's in now if I'd acted when I should."

"Culter can't drive a car? His garage is empty: I don't remember ever seeing him in one."

"If he dies before we get to him—"

"We've got men watching the railway station."

"— if he commits suicide —"

"Is he brave enough?"

"I can't read his mind. I've put myself in another's place once too often. It doesn't work."

"The roads are watched. I rang Headquarters before I came to the cell."

"We might never find him," and the Sergeant had a vision of Culter's body somewhere on the moors, decaying over the years until only its bones remained. "We can't keep Blackoe without bringing him to trial. I can't let him go so long as he won't tell us anything."

Barker walked to the window and looked out, afraid to

believe in the reality of the dawn beginning to creep over the hills, and what was justice? Had he wanted to destroy Cluff to save Blackoe?

It got lighter and he heard the Duty Constable coming to his post in the outer office, relieving the night clerk. The Sergeant had his eyes closed but he wasn't sleeping. Voices on the other side of the door notified the arrival of Mole and they'd forgotten the Inspector.

"What's this?" and the door burst open. "Didn't I say all along Culter killed him?" and the Inspector's face was red with anger. "Doesn't anyone tell me anything? They're my men you're using, my men you've called out—" The look on Barker's face cut him short. He glanced at Cluff, who didn't move, and as he drove him back to the outer office, following him there, Barker clicked the light off before closing the door behind him.

"It was me," Barker said. "All the time the only thing he had in his mind was to spare a man he'd always known, whom he'd been sorry for, whose life he didn't want to make more of a wreck. And it all pointed to Hilda Blackoe. He didn't strain the evidence. He was justified in arriving at the solution he did."

"Because he knew Culter—" Mole began to argue, and the telephone on the counter rang.

Barker knew by the dog that the C.I.D. room door had opened. The Duty Constable had the receiver to his ear, mouthing an occasional monosyllable, making notes with a pencil on a pad. "We'll send someone out," he said, and Cluff was reading what he'd written before he put the telephone down.

"We've got him?" Inspector Mole asked.

Barker looked over the Sergeant's shoulder at the pad: "The quarry?"

"What quarry?" and the Inspector was beside him, reading as well. "Detonators? Gelignite?" and he considered. "A professional job: they'll be a hundred miles away. They won't want it for use in Gunnarshaw."

"Over the moor from my cottage," Cluff said, breaking his silence, "it's no more than three or four miles."

"Not Culter. He wouldn't draw attention to himself like that. If he stole it'd be food or money. What would he blow up with that stuff?" Mole offered, "If you don't want to send Barker, I'll go."

"Do something for me."

"If I can."

"When Blackoe comes up before the magistrates this morning—"

"He's not affected, surely?"

"I'm in no position to prosecute."

"He's pleading guilty."

"Don't let him."

"Me—?" but the Sergeant had already reached the street door and Barker was leaving too.

He stopped a bus in the High Street and Barker and Clive climbed in after him. A couple of miles out of Gunnarshaw a police car drove across the road from a side-lane and one of its crew got out for a word with the conductor but saw the Sergeant through the window and saluted. "Who's the unlucky one?" the conductor asked, as the bus drove off, and he grinned: "That lot's shutting the stable door after the horse has gone, as usual. You're not taking a ride for the sake of your health, Caleb."

"Not only for mine, somebody else's too."

"I'll bet! Whoever it is won't find prison much of a rest-cure when you catch him."

They got off where the hills almost touched the road, rising steeply, often nude of grass like a body of flesh, the white limestone skeleton exposed. A lane roughly macadamed, its surface depressed and cracked by the wheels of heavy lorries, took them through a gap with high, sheer sides, artificially cut, and brought them into an immense excavation. A crushing mill built of corrugated iron, whitened by lime dust, clanked, filling the hollow with its echo, and young conifers had been planted nearer the road where the workings had been abandoned for new diggings farther in. A man dangled at the end of a rope on the face of a cliff, probing at the rock, and mechanical shovels jabbed at a mass of boulders dislodged by a recent blasting. Dust hung suspended in the air and fresh clouds of it billowed constantly, making the atmosphere thicker.

A foreman in a steel helmet took them into the trees, to a square stone building with an iron door, no more than a dozen feet or so square and about as tall. "It's not the main magazine," he explained. "That's nearer the quarry face. We used this when we were beginning, before we moved on: it's an overflow store now." At its back a solid wooden shutter had blocked an unglazed window space and it was rotten with age, its wood spongy. The quarryman had the grace to look ashamed: "Damn it, Caleb, we don't calculate on burglars!"

The shutter hung on its hinges, a crowbar on the ground not far off, and the bolt on the inside had been wrenched from its fastenings.

Cluff poked his head through the hole to look into the store at wooden cases and some metal ones: "What's missing?"

"A handful of detonators. A few sticks of blasting material."

"They didn't take it all."

"They'd have needed a van." The foreman pointed to the track along which they'd come. "No wheel marks." He walked away a short distance to where the ground was wetter: "I'd not have put it past the lads from the village but this chap came by himself." The footprints, before they lost themselves in short, cropped turf, went both ways, up to and down from the rim of the quarry.

They left the foreman there and pulled themselves to the edge where the rock-cutting had started, the land above inclining almost perpendicularly for a while and then easing, barred by a drystone wall from the moor. "Culter?" Barker said, as they made for the skyline, through brittle bracken dying back for the winter.

"It could have been."

"What for?"

"He'd see the telephone in my passage. He'd hardly go back to the town when all we had to do was ring up for men to wait for him."

From the highest point of the moor, the ridge to which both sides climbed, the slope in front of them plunged sharply before levelling gradually into the fields and the pastures in the valley bottom. The Sergeant's cottage nestled in the lee of a spur of ground with the ribbon of road beyond it winding to a distant hill crowned by the first houses of Gunnarshaw, Mole's and Culter's amongst them, the town hidden behind but overhung by a light pall of smoke.

"This would have been the logical way," the Sergeant said, as they descended. "He'd avoid the road. He wouldn't go home."

"After the quarry, where?" Barker replied.

"His tracks started back again."

"There's a hundred places he could hide, amongst the crags, in the plantations, behind the rocks. If he lay down in the bracken we could pass within half a dozen yards of him and never know he was there."

"He'll have to come out sometime," and Cluff sounded happier than he'd done in the police station. He swung along with a step that Barker envied, at a pace not much affected by his two sleepless nights, Clive ranging ahead. Grouse, gobbling, flew from under their feet with a whir of wings: black-faced, thick-fleeced sheep lifted their heads inquisitively, their wary eyes following the movements of the dog.

CHAPTER XVIII

"We're here," Barker said, into the telephone. "At the cottage." He told Mole at the other end of the line, "We came back over the tops," and paused. "The Sergeant thinks it was him."

"At the quarry? What the deuce is his idea?"

"It looks as if he took to the moor a second time," and he heard the Inspector whistle. "Blackoe?"

"Wouldn't say a word to the magistrates. They'd have cited him for contempt of court if there'd been any point in it." The detective-constable started to replace the receiver and heard, "Wait a minute." A few moments passed before Mole continued.

"All right," Barker said. Annie Croft stood in the kitchen doorway at the end of the passage, an expression of concern on her face, and he waited for her to come forward. She nodded her head at the door of the living-room: "He'll never forgive himself. Whatever they've done, the dead don't return."

"That's not the worst of it," he said, thinking of Blackoe. "Nor that he was wrong about Culter." Back with Cluff, he told him, "Superintendent Patterson arrived at the station while I was on the phone. He's on his way out."

In a matter of minutes Annie showed Patterson in and the Sergeant muttered, "You ought to buy a house here: it'd save you travelling backwards and forwards."

"That's better," Annie said, and went into the kitchen to make tea.

"You worried me when I rang you after getting home yesterday. Barker's call early today didn't help," Patterson began. "The whole force is on watch for him."

"He hasn't got that far away."

"I wouldn't have believed it about him any more than you did."

Annie entered with a tray of cups and saucers: "You're both fools. You should have asked a woman what she thought about Culter." She passed round the cups of tea and after she'd left them Patterson said, "Mole told me about the man you've got at the station—" He sat straighter in his chair, changing the subject: "That's not the mill buzz," and looked at his watch. "It isn't five yet."

"The fire siren," Barker explained, listening to the distant, long-drawn-out wail drifting over the fields from Gunnarshaw. Cluff put his cup down and stood up: "Dan—"

"It's a job for the uniformed branch," Patterson objected, and shot a glance at Barker. Something in the detective-constable's face silenced him and he nodded, going after Cluff into the passage, where Annie was on guard. She said, "Look after him," as the Sergeant went outside. "Culter isn't sane."

The Superintendent's big saloon turned out of the lane into the minor road and Barker, in the back with Clive, shut his eyes and braced himself with his feet against the front seat. Their own brakes shrieked in concert with those of the police car and the crash he'd anticipated from the brief glimpse he'd had didn't materialize. He looked again, at a constable running towards them and shouting, the other car with one wheel in the ditch and a wing buried in the hedge. Patterson restarted his engine and pressed hard on the accelerator.

"Right!" Cluff said at the top of the hill where the avenue both Mole and Culter lived in branched off, and, "Left!" at the main road when they reached the corner where Barker had spoken with the postman. He ordered, "Right!" again, forgetting perhaps that Patterson had been born in Gunnarshaw, after a few hundred yards and the Superintendent swung across the carriageway into a side-street curving round the base of a hill and crossed the canal by a swing bridge like the one farther along giving access to the park.

Over the bridge and the towpath the road plunged between a high-walled yard and the side wall of the mill extending some hundreds of yards along the canal bank, first its engine house and then its coal bunkers and furnace room, and finally the storeyed bulk of its weaving sheds and processing rooms and warehousing. Five lines of windows ranged one above the other, each with a doorway at its farther end, opening on to the landing of a red-painted, iron fire-escape. The windows were lit but the mill looked strangely inactive and a uniformed constable held up his hand to stop their car before he recognized its occupants and waved it on. A second constable was posted at the junction with the main road the front of the mill faced.

Traffic had piled up in the direction of the town and Barker could see another line of lorries and buses and cars past the mill lower down, the road between clear but the pavement on the railway side crowded with people other constables were attempting in vain to scatter. A few last operatives ran to join them from the wide mill entrance, towards which Patterson drove.

They got out and ran through the gates into a yard inset in the mass of the building, surrounded by it on three sides. Its black-helmeted crew circled a fire-appliance and craned their necks towards shattered windows on one of the upper storeys but there was neither smoke nor flame nor any smell of burning.

Inspector Mole turned to meet them: "He's in there."

"You haven't let him get through the town without anyone stopping him?" Patterson demanded.

"Ask the watchman," and Mole pointed to a man sheltering in an archway beside a bank of time-clocks. "He's just arrived to see the fun."

"Where's the fire?"

"There isn't one. Not yet."

The man by the time clocks stuttered with excitement. "I didn't know," he protested, "and I've been asleep all day. I'm on nights. Culter was about early this morning before it got light. Nobody told me you wanted him."

"There's a door near the furnace room on the canal bank," the Inspector interrupted. "Once in he could have hidden all day, in a lavatory, changing his spot maybe. He knows the place: he's worked there all his life."

A fireman shouted and a figure appeared at one of the broken windows. "He's gone off his head," Mole stated. "He turned up about half an hour ago in the packing room and they couldn't get near him."

The Superintendent exclaimed, "There must be a labour force of hundreds."

"There is. It's a wonder some of them are alive. You know what he stole last night. He got the packing staff as far as the door and then blew a hole in the floor between him and them to speed their departure. When I turned up after sending the police car to tell you he was yelling his head off, threatening to go through the whole place and send it to Kingdom-come piecemeal. We cleared the mill and called the brigade to stand by."

"Bright!" Cluff cupped his hands round his mouth and the walls of the yard caught his voice, bouncing it back. The murmur of the crowd lessened and ceased. "Bright!" he yelled. "Bright!"

"Come and get me," a voice answered, distantly.

"You'll have to come out."

"Who says I want to?"

The crowd in the road started to chatter again. "He'll do it," the Inspector said. "There's two hundred thousand pounds worth of property there. He's got it at his mercy."

The C.I.D. Superintendent turned on him: "The place has half-a-dozen entrances. You've plenty of men. Split them up. Send all your parties in together."

"He's done enough damage already," the manager intervened, appearing from an office behind the time-clocks. "At the very least he could stop production for weeks."

"You're an optimist," a fireman said. "If he picks his spot to start a blaze you'll be out of business for good."

Cluff set off for the main door and, "I'll go with you," Patterson was saying when Culter shouted, "Don't, Caleb! It isn't you I want."

Someone remarked, "He's always been clever with his

hands. He'll know how to set things up. It'd be suicide."

"Every day," Culter shouted, "for over thirty years, every single day, this place, going home to what, coming here to what? Two weeks off in summer, but when could I go away for a holiday? Always back to it: always home to that!"

"You tell me," the Inspector pleaded generally. "What is there except to shoot him? And he'd still have time. What happens if we get in there? Somebody's going to get killed. I'd be as big a murderer as he is to send my men after him. He's nothing to lose and he knows it." He looked at Cluff. "You've got some queer friends. If you'd listened to me—"

"I'll make a bargain with you," Culter's voice came from the window. "He did it. If it hadn't been for him you wouldn't have known."

Which of them? Every man in the yard had his eyes on Cluff.

"Barker," the voice called, with a break in it, choking on a sob. "He's the one. It was all over, finished, until he started it again."

"You've worked with them," the Sergeant replied. "You can't put them out of a job."

"You took me home with you. You were sorry for me."

Cluff pleaded with all the urgency he could: "Bright—"

"They've all laughed at me. They've always laughed at me. Send him in."

"Come out. I'll look after you."

"I'm taking him with me. Send him in!" and Culter disappeared from view.

The Sergeant stepped in front of Barker: "If this is anybody's job, it's mine."

"You heard what he said," and Barker turned to the Chief

Superintendent. "It's the only way."

"For doing your duty?" Cluff burst out. "For finding the letters I should have looked for?"

"We'll starve him out," Patterson proposed.

"My schedules," the manager groaned. "I've got orders to meet."

"They've a canteen in there," Cluff said.

"Cut the water off!"

"And the sprinklers," the manager wanted to know, "if he starts a fire?"

A dull rumble inside the mill cut them all short, mingling with a gasp from the crowd in the road, followed by the tattoo of feet as it began to disintegrate, running for safety. The brief flash behind windows to their right that had still been intact made them blink and glass tumbled on the floor of the yard. The voice rose over the other sounds, "Send him in! Send him in!" and silence followed, only to be broken by a loud crash as of something heavy collapsing. The manager wrung his hands: "You can't let him do it!"

"We're all going in," and Patterson went back to his original plan. "By every door there is."

"The size of the place," Mole protested. "We'd need an army."

"Let me try," Barker begged.

"He'll kill you together with himself."

"I'll talk to him."

"He's past listening."

"If I don't, how many is he going to take with him, how many are going to get hurt? It's one man, or a dozen maybe, more than that—"

CHAPTER XIX

The men holding Cluff released him and he faced the Chief Superintendent: "You know what you've done?"

"You think I like it? But Barker was right. It's him or God knows how many. We'll pray that Culter sees reason."

"You shouldn't have asked it."

"Barker's a policeman. The job has its risks. You'd have gone in instead of him if we'd let you."

"I've had my life. His is just beginning."

"And Mole's men have wives and children."

The Sergeant's big body drooped and he leaned heavily on his stick. Clive took up a position close to him, joining him in defiance of the enemy. They were all his enemies, Patterson, the Inspector, the constables, the firemen, all of them congregated in the yard, who'd let Barker go and used physical force to prevent him from interfering. He walked to the gates and two of them accompanied him, wary eyes on the dog. The opposite side of the road was clear of workpeople, who massed now at either end of the long mill, where the lines of traffic were longer in both directions.

He turned back into the yard, Clive close to him, still followed, the mill very quiet, a thin plume of smoke eddying from the scene of the last explosion, dispersing in the dusk. Lights shone through every window, left burning when the place was evacuated, row upon row of them, serried ranks of yellow. "Up there," a voice said, and an arm pointed at the outline of a human figure.

"Barker!"

It appeared and disappeared, in this window and that, on one storey after another, climbing from floor to floor, showing itself deliberately at intervals to the yard below in order to indicate its progress. Interest as to where it would appear next mounted, overcoming to some extent and temporarily, their concern about its ultimate fate. The dusk had deepened and the waiting men merged and lost identity, crowded together, every eye on the windows, every neck stretched, heads lifted. Occasionally Clive whimpered and from out of the night the impatient blast of a car horn sounded, some driver arriving at the end of the queue, not yet in the picture and angry at the interruption of his journey. They whispered to each other, expressing their fears and their hopes, while the Sergeant sidled to the fire-truck and stood against it in the darker shadows.

"How long?" and Inspector Mole asked the question in all their minds. "What's Culter's idea? He wanted Barker in there. He's got him. Why doesn't he stay where he can be found?"

The windows seemed to have been blank for hours and they almost began to believe the mill deserted, that perhaps Culter had slipped away through one of its many exits. A single man could take all night to search the huge building and he'd never be sure that he hadn't missed his object, amongst the banks of looms in the weaving sheds, the piles of finished products in the stores, the machinery and the benches, the interconnecting rooms, the lifts and hoists and staircases.

A murmur went up from the unseen crowd in the road but nobody turned his head or took his eyes away from those rows of lights surrounding them on three sides.

Patterson sighed, the responsibility his, and he was the man in the early days of Barker's career, after the time when Cluff had stood firm in the matter of Amy Wright's death,[*] who'd approved the young constable's application for transfer from the uniformed branch to the C.I.D. What option had he had but to let Barker go, yet how could he weigh human lives in the balance against each other? He couldn't hear what they were saying in the road, as they watched Cluff slinking in the shelter of the mill wall, with Clive at his heels, the remarks about himself and Mole, the hopes that now the Sergeant was on the move again things might begin to happen. He'd forgotten Cluff in the stress of his thoughts, in the absence of further protests during this interval of waiting, and so had the men with him, too preoccupied, too concerned with those windows to notice the Sergeant's stealthy progress, stopping and starting, noiseless, from where he'd been standing reconciled by the fire-truck to the gate, round its corner.

The Sergeant's step quickened. The constable at the junction where the side road turned off to the canal, without orders to the contrary, didn't dream of hindering him. He climbed the slope with Clive, to the canal bank, and they hurried along it past the engine room and the coal bunkers.

He reached up with his walking stick and hooked the lowest rung of the bottom ladder on the fire escape, dragging it down on its spring-balanced hinge. He pushed himself through the gap in the first landing and, after glancing through the glass

[*]   *Sergeant Cluff Stands Firm*

panels of the fire door opening on to it, through the second landing and the third, mounting higher and higher, the canal, black and glistening, narrowing beneath him. Approaching the roof of the building he could hear more clearly the disturbance in the yard on the other side. He couldn't stop whatever action Patterson was taking if he'd discovered him gone: he could only hope that it wouldn't end in disaster. He wasn't sure himself how wise he was being, whether he wouldn't make matters worse and cause more harm than he intended but to leave Barker in the lurch any longer was unthinkable. His blindness about Culter had been purged: the scales had fallen from his eyes: he couldn't make men what he would have them by thinking them so. He wondered how far the housekeeper or the weaver, that little, shy, meek man, was responsible for what had been between them.

The escape didn't go any higher and the eaves were just above him. Clive's paws scraped on the netted mesh of the iron treads and when he glanced at the dog it was trembling but persistent, afraid of the height yet determined. He hadn't wanted it to follow and he would have sent Clive back to the ground if the descent hadn't been more beyond the dog's capacity than the climb.

He tried the fire door, with the wind whistling round him on his isolated platform, as far into the clouds, probably, as he could get anywhere in Gunnarshaw without actually flying. A bolt or a latch, as he'd expected, held it secure on the inside. He didn't want to make a noise but he'd no other way in and he lifted his stick and crashed it into the glass. He knocked the jagged edges still adhering to the frame away and found the bolt with the arm he thrust through.

They stood, the man and the dog, at the end of a long space occupying the entire width of the building, divided into bays by round pillars supporting the ceiling and the rafters above it, crammed with great baskets holding bobbins and the kind of stiff cardboard tubes wound round with yarn he and his friends had used for peashooters when they were boys. The wide shaft of a hoist gaped at him, toothed with a collapsible grille, and two-wheeled sack-carts were parked haphazardly about, cheek by jowl with low-platformed four-wheeled trollies railed at only one end.

He held his breath to sharpen his hearing. The windows shut out whatever sounds were being made outside and the mill seemed very silent. It took an effort to realize that somewhere in its vastness one man pursued another, and which of them was hunted or which the hunter? Did the lure entice the tracker to an inevitable ambush? Had it ended already?

The stolen explosives filled his mind. He knew little about their qualities and had fuses and a firing-box, too, been missing from the store at the quarry? He tried not to think, as he crossed the floor to closed double doors at the far end of the room, that Culter had had time, early this morning or during the exodus of the millhands, to prepare his shots. Had the man nothing to remember that he didn't hate and want to destroy, no memory at all of joys, however transitory, now that the one dream he'd almost realized had burst like a bubble in his face? Wasn't there any place existing that held for him a recollection of happiness? Had the years of his experience here been as hard as those parts of them he'd had to spend in the house on the hill, looked down on by his neighbours, tied to an old woman, ostracized for his calling and envied for his mother's money? Everywhere the same, ridiculed, scorned instead of praised for the family duty he hadn't been able to avoid, that he'd been too weak to free himself from, dominated at home, a figure of fun at work.

Vaguely, as the Sergeant went from room to room, he became aware of movement far down in the depths under his feet. Clive's paws pattered on the wooden floors, greasy with the accumulated rubbing of raw cotton. He had his heart in his mouth and a feeling of panic grew stronger, dragging him towards a frantic wildness in his search that he knew would surely defeat its purpose. His skin rose into goose-lumps: his ears strained for the initial warning. Would he hear it first or before he heard it would the walls cave in around him and the floors collapse, plunging him and a confusion of masonry headlong amongst crashing machinery down into the foundations of the building, to be buried irrevocably in a mass of rubble? He became more and more certain that all he'd accomplished was the ruin of his friends and comrades, Patterson, Mole, the men he'd worked with at the station, which it had been Barker's intention to avoid. He knew, with an utter hopelessness, that while they'd been prepared to wait for the outcome of the detective-constable's sacrifice they'd moved into action for him. Far from being grateful, or honoured, he cursed them for their rashness, their lack of sense, their idiocy.

He wasn't walking any longer, he was running, with Clive panting beside him, careless of noise, doors banging behind him, raising the echoes, unable to assess how much time remained, whether there was any time at all. He lost all sense of direction. Now he went up, now down, boots clattering, in an eeriness the glare of the electric bulbs only heightened. He existed in a nightmare, caught up in an endless search he was doomed to continue for ever, the threat of obliteration never farther away than the next second.

He jerked to a halt, disbelieving, a door swinging behind him. Rank after rank of looms, misshapen robots waiting to pounce, stood to attention for the word of attack, silent, menacing. Barker, white-faced, crouched halfway down an alley, staring in his direction but not at him. Voices, not close, a long way off, were shouting his name and he was shouting Barker's.

He saw Culter begin to turn as the dog leapt past him for the hunched shoulders and he was so near to the man's back he could almost have reached him without moving. He didn't know whether he could move, growing from the spot, rooted there, and whatever came of it he'd never have any recollection of launching himself forwards, of becoming mixed with the man and the dog, of snatching at an arm beginning to lift just as the fingers on the hand at the end of it were starting to open. He thought, with his last thought, that something small and dark, aimed originally at him, went curving in a long, soaring parabola, its intended course frustrated at the very moment it was parting from Culter's grip. He glimpsed, in a flash of sight, Barker diving full-length between the looms for the floor. He heard Clive yelp and the drive of air from Culter's lungs as they tumbled in a heap, a heaving softness of flesh and fur underneath him.

The universe blew itself apart, falling to pieces, with a brilliance at once succeeded by a blinding dark, with a roar replaced by an absolute quiet, in a rain of debris and a bombardment of missiles that stopped as suddenly as it had begun. It wasn't Culter he was glad, in that last moment, he was shielding with his body, his final reaction one of thanks that his back protected the dog.

CHAPTER XX

Faces filled his vision like those of drowned men seen through the reeds of a lake, wavering, approaching a substance never quite attained, fading, half visible again before the ripples sent them deeper. Voices spoke in whispers, a conversation of ghosts, their tone conveying something he couldn't quite catch, their words indistinguishable. There was a whiteness in the world that worried him, too clean, too unnatural, too immaterial. He couldn't think. He didn't know where he was. Did pain continue after death and wasn't there ever any release?

It went on and on, the faces changing, but the same ones coming back over and over again. This transformation of his limbs, this imprisonment of their motion, these ungainly garments in which he seemed to be swathed, these gentle hands fluttering about him – was it, then, like this? Not frightening, not cruel, and the pain decreasing, from a knife-cut to a throb, from a throb to nothing.

His vision cleared, not all at once, but gradually, and his heart contracted. Had he brought them with him too, Patterson, Mole, Barker in a white turban, even Annie Croft, who shouldn't be there at all? What reason had they to smile when the fault was his, when he'd involved them in the chaos that had led to this? The dog too, more pathetic because more defenceless, like Blackoe, relying on its human masters and failed in its final hour.

"He's coming to," and the lips belonged to someone he believed he recognized but who had even less right to be there than the others, Doctor Hamm also an intruder. But it wasn't worth it, these questions, this self-inquiry, this personal inquisition. This time he let them go for good and closed his eyes, a peace in sleep, or in death, it didn't matter which.

"A woman," he thought, and remembered Hilda Blackoe, and the woman in the attic, and women on street corners. This one didn't look like that and he was prepared to give her the benefit of the doubt, young and sweet, but how could he ever be sure about people again? Her lips parted and she laughed: "The Inspector said so." She paused a moment. "That you were indestructible."

The room wasn't his, nor the bed, nor the pyjamas he wore instead of his customary nightshirt. He lifted himself higher on the pillow and groped for the bedclothes with an arm clumsy with bandages.

"Oh no," she objected, "you don't," and tucked him up again like a baby.

He gave her best for the time being and accepted the drink she held to his mouth but he stored up his resentment for future reference. He slept again and woke and slept some more, and then sunlight was shining on a polished floor and the smell was antiseptic.

"Better?" the nurse asked.

"You can't keep me here."

She went to the door. "Help," she called, and her voice

was amused. It brought Annie Croft in. "You were right," the nurse said.

"What did I tell you?" Annie replied and crossed to Cluff's bedside. "You'll stop there," she stated, "until they say you can go, if I have to make them tie you down."

"I ought to have known you'd a hand in it."

"As soon as you get out of my sight—"

"Barker?" he asked, suddenly.

The nurse put her head out of the room a second time and Barker was there, a bandage round his head, with Clive, and then Patterson and Mole.

"Get me out of this place," Cluff ordered, and they didn't reply. "Whose side are you on?"

"We ought to have locked you up," Mole said.

"It's as well you didn't," Barker interrupted. "I couldn't do anything with Culter."

"He's still alive?" the Sergeant asked.

"It wasn't too bad, after all," Patterson told him. "There'll be some repairs to do but they'll manage. The brigade cleared up for them."

"You weren't far away."

"On the stairs. Too near for my liking."

"Where is he?"

"Here."

"Hurt?"

"A bit. He was under you, like Clive. You make a better door than a window."

"He's talked?" and Cluff sat up. "What have they done with my clothes?"

"They're not daft enough," Annie said, "to leave them

lying about where you can get at them."

"If that's the case," and Cluff threw the covers back.

They called the Sister and the Matron but in the end they gave him a dressing-gown and put him in a wheelchair. They pushed him along the corridor and into a small room where Culter lay in a bed with a uniformed constable on guard. "Leave me alone with him," the Sergeant said.

Culter's bright, fevered eyes bored into Cluff and his lips twisted. He'd lost his hangdog look and his meekness of manner and the real man showed through.

"We've known each other a long time," Cluff said, "almost since we were both born. You weren't running away when we found you in the fields because she was still alive."

"You won't rest," Culter replied, "till you have the whole of it. You never do."

The Sergeant studied him and they could hear the movement outside in the corridor. Culter said at last, "She didn't see me kill that man in the garden but she guessed, who it was and that I'd done it."

"So that he wouldn't trouble her again?"

"And then Mole showed her the photograph. I didn't know what she was really like. I couldn't believe what I read in the letters."

"Afterwards?"

"She kept being ill – I told you that. I couldn't stop thinking about her. I knew the baby wasn't mine. I thought about it all day at the mill and when I got home she didn't care that I'd made up my mind not to marry her. And I might still have forgiven her, even the child, but she was confident, because she knew what I'd done to Todd. She threatened to come to you. She mocked me and laughed at me. She said I couldn't have married her anyway, not legally, because she'd a husband still alive, but it didn't matter because if I wanted her to keep quiet I'd have to look after her for as long as she wished. She'd make me go through a ceremony and I'd never get rid of her. I'd have to keep the child as well and any others she had, mine or not."

"You had the knife."

"I hadn't been able to throw it away. It always seemed I'd find another occasion to use it." He lay back against the pillow. "Until Barker came to the cottage—"

"You'd have let her husband take the blame?"

"What are people to me, after the way they've treated me?" He leaned forward again. "I'd have done it if I could: I'd have destroyed the mill. I'd have killed Barker, you too, if you'd got in my way."

Cluff put his hands on the grips of the chair. He wheeled it backwards to the door and kicked on the panels till Barker opened it, the constable and Patterson and Mole, Annie and Clive behind him. The Sergeant nodded at Bright Culter: "He'll make a statement. Get it down on paper. When you read it you'll know what to do with Blackoe." Only Barker didn't stare at him or fail to understand when he added, "Another man for whom life wasn't worth living but he'll get over it in time." He looked at them and added, "His wife was dead when he got there. If he had the knife in his hands it was because he pulled it out of her. Bring him to the cottage before you let him leave Gunnarshaw. I'd like to talk to him, not as a policeman—"

"The cottage!" Annie exclaimed, throwing up her hands

in despair.

"And now those clothes."

"You're not getting them."

"Then I'll walk through the streets without them. It'll be a sight for Gunnarshaw's sore eyes."

They capitulated but not before they'd called in the hospital doctor. "Life won't be worth living for any of us if he stays," he said. "I'll let him go providing he'll stop in bed and promise to take an ambulance home."

Doctor Hamm said from behind them, "It won't be necessary. I've brought my car. It's outside."

"So I've one friend," the Sergeant muttered, and corrected himself, stroking Clive, "Two."

"Give me a hand with him," Hamm asked Barker. "I've put his clothes in the car. It's not worth dressing him."

"I'll be along to see you, Caleb," Patterson promised, at the same time as Mole was telling Annie, "I'll come and sit with him if you can't be there all the time. My wife'll help too."

"You all coddle him. The more he gets his own way the more he wants it."

She looked at Cluff in the hope of raising a smile but his face remained dull and she turned away, tossing her head and sniffing noisily.

The next Cluff…

Sergeant Cluff Laughs Last

Detective-Sergeant Cluff, from the shadows of a ginnel, watches a young woman weeping in Gunnarshaw's busy high street – and wonders why. But when a dead body is discovered in a forest plantation, Cluff calls on his extensive knowledge of Gunnarshaw folk, as well as his instinctive perception of human nature, to uncover a trail of fateful and unrequited love.

As the investigation progresses, nothing is as it seems, and as Cluff knows only too well from a lifetime of detective work, when it comes to crimes of passion, there are never any easy answers. Inspector Mole, on the other hand, is certain he has the case all wrapped up – and is determined to prove Cluff wrong.

by the same author

Published by The British Library

SERGEANT CLUFF STANDS FIRM
THE METHODS OF SERGEANT CLUFF

Published by Great Northern Books

SERGEANT CLUFF GOES FISHING
MORE DEATHS FOR SERGEANT CLUFF
SERGEANT CLUFF LAUGHS LAST

www.gnbooks.co.uk